"I DIDN'T SEE MARK . . ."

Mary's voice was shaky. Her arms tightened around me. "How could I have been with him when I was with you, Cath?"

I know that Mary felt my body stiffen, and I buried my head against her shoulder so that her mother couldn't see my face. I hadn't even had a chance to deal with the knowledge that a friend, someone Mary loved, was dead, and now Mary was lying. Why? What was I going to do? I didn't want Mark to be dead. And I didn't want Mary to be lying about where she'd been . . .

One Step Short

Jane McFann

AN AVON  FLARE BOOK

ONE STEP SHORT is an original publication of Avon Books. This work has never before appeared in book form.

AVON BOOKS
A division of
The Hearst Corporation
105 Madison Avenue
New York, New York 10016

Copyright © 1990 by Jane McFann
Front cover photograph by Abe Rezny
Published by arrangement with the author
Library of Congress Catalog Card Number: 89-91866
ISBN: 0-380-75805-9
RL: 5.4

First Avon Flare Printing: April 1990

AVON FLARE TRADEMARK REG. U.S. PAT. OFF. AND IN OTHER COUNTRIES, MARCA REGISTRADA, HECHO EN U.S.A.

Printed in the U.S.A.

RA 10 9 8 7 6 5 4 3 2 1

To my parents, for their love

To my niece, Kristin Collins, for whom I wish nothing but happy endings

And to Jim Shepherd, for being the first person to encourage me to write

Chapter 1

Bulldozer Boy came back in October. No, *Robert* came back. I had vowed never to think of him as Bulldozer Boy, a cruel nickname given to him by kids at my school because he charged through the halls, head down, body hunched, knocking down anybody in his way. All the months he had been there, he had never spoken, never said a single word until he said goodbye to me, a single word that had nearly broken my heart.

I had vowed to find him, to try to make him give me one more chance to understand what had turned him into that Bulldozer Boy, but I had failed. I had called, written, contacted every person I could think of, yet I had never found him.

Now he was standing at my door on a crisp Delaware Saturday morning.

It was 10:30, and I was still in my pink flowered nightgown. It wasn't that I was still in bed; it's just that sometimes it's a real struggle for me to put on actual clothes when my nightgown is all flannelly and warm and comfortable. I also had on slippers with high furry cuffs that came up around my ankles. Yes, I know—a true fashionplate. Still, it was a fine outfit for what I'd been doing—easing into the day by reading, dozing, and daydreaming until I gradually became mobile.

When the doorbell rang, I snarled. I was leaning against the counter in the kitchen, finishing a mug of hot chocolate, contemplating getting dressed and getting a true start on the day when that irritating "dong" interrupted my thoughts. (The doorbell is supposed to go "ding dong" but the "ding" died years ago and Mom and I never got it fixed.)

I looked down at my outfit and started for my bedroom, not too quickly, I admit. I figured it was the paperboy collecting, and he could wait a minute or two. I considered changing into sweats but settled for my old blue terry cloth robe, which I belted over my nightgown as I walked back to the door. The bell donged again as I got near it.

"Okay, okay. I'm coming," I said irritably. I turned the deadbolt lock and flung open the door, looking down in anticipation of the paperboy's urchin face. Instead my eyes met a substantial chest, and my eyes quickly roved up to a face. Bulldozer Boy's face. No. Robert Sullivan's face.

I'm sure my face reflected my amazement. I could feel my eyes widen and my jaw drop. I couldn't take my eyes off of his face, couldn't say a word. I saw a trace of an uncertain smile tug at the corners of his mouth, and I knew I had to shake myself into action.

"I can't believe it's you," I said, then suddenly realized that wasn't exactly a warm welcome. "I'm glad it is you, but I'm just surprised, that's all," I babbled. He continued to look at me uncertainly. "Come in," I said, suddenly afraid that he would turn around and run and that I'd have to go chasing him in my nightgown. There was no way I was going to let him get away again without having a chance to talk to him. I put out a hand, ready to grab his arm if he started to leave, but then jerked it back, remembering how much he hated to be touched, hated to even have anyone near him.

"Are you sure it's all right if I come in?" I stared at him in amazement. His voice was soft and husky, but he was definitely talking.

"Yes, I'm positive. Please. You have to come in. Don't you dare try to leave."

With that eloquent welcome, he stepped inside the door and stood there uncertainly. "Come into the living room and sit down," I said. "Would you like some hot chocolate? Some coffee? Tea?" Please say yes, I mentally begged him. Give me a chance to compose myself.

"Yes. Hot chocolate's fine." he said quietly, settling into the corner of the sofa.

"Great," I said, sprinting for the kitchen. "That's great."

I filled a large glass measuring cup with water and put it in the microwave to heat, then took out two packets of hot chocolate mix and found two clean mugs. That under control, I dashed through the living room, past the still-startled looking Robert, and into my bedroom. In a single movement my robe was unbelted and dropped on the floor and my nightgown was whipped over my head as I stepped out of my slippers. A hasty search found me a pair of navy blue sweat pants, an oversized red sweat shirt, and a pair of red and blue striped socks. Just as I started to desperately pull a brush through my hair, I heard the microwave beep. I looked at my face in the mirror, shook my head, and dashed back through the living room.

It's a wonder that I made it from the kitchen to the coffee table without spilling one or both mugs of hot chocolate, but I did. I sat his in front of him, then put mine at the opposite end, throwing myself into the large chair that sat at a right angle to the sofa. I didn't want to get too close to Robert, didn't want to scare him away.

"Thank you," he said.

"Oh, it's nothing. It's just instant, but we don't have the real stuff, only the fake stuff." Again I was babbling.

"Thank you for trying to find me," he said. It took Robert to focus us on something that mattered.

"I had to," I said. "I couldn't stand for you to think that I was as bad as all of the rest of the people who made your life miserable."

"I knew that," he said, his voice still very soft and husky, as if he were just recovering from laryngitis.

"I've done a lot of thinking about why kids are so cruel to anyone who's different," I continued. "They don't try to find out why a person is different. They just tear down someone else to boost themselves. Deep down inside, they're scared to death that someone's going to mock them, so they mock someone else real fast before they become targets themselves. That's not what I did," I added, needing to defend myself just a little. "It's not that I ridiculed you, because I didn't. It's more that I didn't do enough to try to help. I didn't understand in time."

Robert looked at me searchingly. "It was my fault anyway," he said. "I didn't give anyone a chance to understand me. How are people supposed to understand a Bulldozer Boy who rams through them as if they're invisible?"

I knew he had to have heard that name thrown at

4

him time after time, but it hurt to hear it spoken in his own voice.

"That's the best you could do right then," I said, finding that I was speaking as softly as he was.

"I have to try to do better," he replied. There was a pause, a silence that stretched between us. The words came slowly, sounding like they were being ripped out of him one by one. "I need your help."

Chapter 2

"I need to find an apartment."

"An apartment," I repeated, nodding. If he wanted an apartment, I'd find him one. I didn't know how, but I'd do it. I'd build one if I had to. "Fine," I said. "We'll find you one. What kind of an apartment would you like?" I sounded like a real estate agent.

"Small and furnished," Robert said.

"Small and furnished," I repeated, nodding my head. "A small and furnished apartment. No problem. There must be hundreds of those around." As my voice rambled on, the real me was having an anxiety attack inside my head. An apartment? it said in panic. What the heck do I know about finding an apartment? How can he do this? He's not old enough to do this. I'm not old enough to help him do this. "Would you prefer one in any particular area of town?" I heard my voice say.

"Somewhere around here," he answered.

"This is a very nice section," I said. "Low crime rate, close to stores, good choice."

"Aren't you going to ask me how I can do this?" Robert's voice interrupted me before I could continue with any more inane statements.

"How can you do this?" The real estate agent was gone, and I was back to being Cath Berry, one very confused teenager.

Robert turned away, facing the wall in front of him rather than me. "After my father was killed, a bunch of people raised reward money to help get information about the case."

He stopped, and I was afraid he wasn't going to continue. "I read about that in the paper," I said softly. "After you left, I did some research."

"The money was put into a trust fund for me. I was supposed to get it at eighteen to help pay for college, but Dr. Epperson convinced the trustees to let me have some of it now so that I could come back here and finish my senior year. She really put herself on the line for me."

"You've been back in Connecticut since you left here?" I asked.

"Yes," Robert answered. "Part of the time I was on my own, part of the time I was with Dr. Epperson."

That must mean that he had been back in the mental institution where he had stayed after his father's death, after he had stopped talking. As I tried to find the right words to ask him about that, he interrupted my thoughts.

"Could we try to find an apartment? Everything I own is outside right now in my car."

I snapped back to the practicalities of the day. "Let's start here," I said. My mother and I had moved into these apartments after she and my father had gotten a divorce. "The rental office is three buildings down." I sprang out of the chair and grabbed my keys off of the hook near the door. Robert followed me to the door, and I locked it behind us.

"Might you be more comfortable with shoes on?" Robert's calm voice startled me. I looked down at my striped socks in amazement.

"Right," I said, my cheeks flushing in embarrassment. I unlocked the door, ran to my bedroom, and shoved Reeboks onto my feet.

There was a trace of a smile on Robert's face when I rejoined him, once again locking the door. I quickly looked down at my body to see if I'd forgotten any other strategic items and was reassured to see that at least I was thoroughly covered. It only took us a few minutes to walk to the office, and the chilly air felt like it was sharpening my mind, thank heavens.

"Yes?" said the lady at the desk. She smiled in my direction; I was often the one who brought in the rent check on the first of the month.

"Do you have any small furnished apartments?" I asked pleasantly.

"And why are you asking?" the lady said sharply. "Does your mother know about this?" Great, I thought. Make me look like a ten-year-old, why don't you?

"It's for me," Robert said in his husky voice.

"I see. And how old are you, may I ask?"

"Old enough to be able to pay for an eight-month lease in advance," Robert said firmly.

"It is our policy to require that you be of legal age, and that you have a verifiable credit rating."

"If you have an apartment that suits me, I can provide you with a reference who will answer all of your questions," Robert said, still speaking softly and calmly.

"I see," snapped the woman. "We only have a few one-bedroom furnished apartments, and they are all rented at the moment. I might have something around December."

"That won't do," Robert responded, turning to leave.

"Just a minute," I said. "May I?" I asked, pointing to the telephone book on her desk. Without waiting for an answer, I picked it up and turned to the Yellow Pages. I appropriated a notepad and pencil also laying on her desk, and began jotting down the names of other apartment complexes in the area.

"You say you have the money to pay the rent in advance?" the lady suddenly asked.

"Thank you for your help," Robert said, moving toward the door. I couldn't tell if there was sarcasm in his voice or not.

"I suddenly thought of something," she said. "One of our tenants was transferred out of town, and I might be able to sublet his to you. Let me see." She typed a name onto the computer screen that faced here. "His lease runs until July."

"I only plan to stay through the middle of June."

Back and forth went Robert and the lady, negotiating when he could get in, when he could leave, how the rent would be paid, who would verify that he could legally do this. My head was spinning after two minutes, but Robert remained focused. Ultimately everything came down to the rental agent calling Dr. Epperson on Monday morning, and Robert getting a cashier's check for a very large sum of money. Finally Robert ended up with a key so that we could take a look at the object of all this talk.

I was silent as we crossed two blocks to get to the far edge of the complex. Robert's face was calm, and he walked briskly. I almost had to jog to keep

9

up. I was slightly out of breath when we finally found Building G, Apartment 11. Robert put the key in the door and pushed it open. I looked around in dismay. The carpet was that puke green sculptured stuff that you never see except in apartments. The walls were white, scuffed in places, and bearing outlines where pictures had once hung. The sofa and chairs were brown and worn, and the drapes that covered the sliding glass doors to the balcony were beige. The end tables and coffee table had white rings on their surfaces. The kitchen was tiny and windowless, and a quick search through the cabinets revealed some chipped dishes with orange flowers on them, a few pans, and some cheap-looking silverware.

I followed Robert to the small bedroom, which contained a bed on a metal frame and a bureau. Off of it was a bathroom, tiled in pink.

All in all, it was one of the most depressing places I had ever seen. Whoever decorated it must have shopped at garage sales.

"What do you think?" Robert asked, looking at me carefully.

"Well, it's . . . adequate," I said, searching for a diplomatic word.

With that, Robert began to laugh, at first more of a choked snuffle but finally a full-fledged laugh. It sounded like he was out of practice. I stared at him in amazement for a moment, but then I began to laugh with him. "It's grotesque," he finally said.

"We can check some other apartment complexes," I said. "There must be something a little more attractive than this." With that, I threw myself down on the sofa, which creaked threateningly.

"No, it's perfect," Robert said, sitting in one of

the chairs. The bottom of it sank until he was almost sitting on the floor. "It's so ugly that it almost has class."

"The best of the worst?" I asked.

"Exactly," he said. "But I need to leave now. I think it needs to be adjusted to in small doses."

We walked back to the rental office and returned the key. Robert promised to check back with the woman on Monday.

We went back toward my apartment, and in the parking lot Robert walked over to a slightly battered yellow Volkswagen Rabbit that was filled to the roof with boxes, bags, and suitcases. He leaned against it, then looked at me. "All my worldly possessions," he said. "Now you need to tell me where I can find a cheap motel for two nights. This car has gotten me here from Connecticut, but I don't exactly want to sleep in it."

The words were out of my mouth before I thought them through. "You can stay with me."

"No, I can't," Robert said. "What would your mother think?"

"She's not home," I replied. "She won't be back for two more weeks."

Chapter 3

As Robert and I lugged his belongings up to my apartment, I filled him in on the latest developments in the Berry family. My parents had divorced years ago, and my father had then voluntarily transferred to Saudi Arabia, only to return last year. That had been a pretty tense time, because he had suddenly tried to reclaim me and force me to live with him and had said that my mother was unfit, which was an absolute laugh. My mother is a lawyer, and what caused all the uproar was that this very nice if slightly boring colleague of hers named Mr. Donelly had moved in with us. Robert was bug-eyed by the time I had explained to him that my father had wanted to date my mother but that she was in love with Mr. Donelly whom she ended up marrying a week ago. It had been a very quiet ceremony in the Justice of the Peace's office with just the three of us, and now Mom and Mr. Donelly were honey-mooning in Ireland, which was why I could invite Robert to stay for two days.

The story and our trekking up and down the steps ended at about the same time. All of Robert's belongings were piled in a heap in the middle of the living room floor, and I threw myself into the chair while he sprawled on the sofa. He was staring at me with a bemused look on his face.

"And all of this is okay with you?" he asked.

"You mean my mother and father and Mr. Donelly and Ireland? Sure. Why not? I figure they're adults, and it's up to them to sort this all out. I just kind of watch." Actually, that wasn't fully true. My mother had consulted me every step of the way to make sure that I wasn't going to be damaged in some bizarre fashion. I had assured her that I was still good old level-headed Cath, and that I loved her even if she did have a more interesting social life than I did.

"She let you stay here alone while she's gone?" Robert asked.

"It took rounds and rounds of negotiation, but finally, yes," I answered. Actually, the original plan had been for me to stay with my father for the three weeks she and Mr. Donelly would be gone. Then my father had gotten an emergency summons to Los Angeles where he was supposed to help reorganize a divisional office that had been cast into chaos because an earthquake had caused structural damage to its headquarters. My mother had tried to insist that I stay with Mary, my best friend whose parents she has known for years, but I convinced her that I was responsible enough at seventeen to manage on my own, knowing that I always had Mary's parents as a backup if anything went wrong. Besides, I'd never get any studying done with Mary; if the truth be known, I was probably safer on my own. It's not that Mary's a bad influence or anything, but she likes constant activity to keep from getting bored.

It was finally my near-perfect record as a responsible daughter that swayed my mother. The only time she had worried about me was while I was dating Tony, and that had ended nearly a year ago. Tony, my brooding, troubled first love.

"Would your mother let me stay if she were home?" Robert asked, jolting me back to the present.

"I think so," I answered. "Besides, she trusts my judgment. I'm hungry," I said, abruptly changing the subject. "Let's order a pizza." I was halfway to the phone on the kitchen wall before I heard him agree. "Extra cheese and mushrooms?" I called to him as I dialed.

"Sure," he agreed.

I ordered a large pizza and fixed us each a glass of cola. I gathered together plates, napkins, and knives for what was either a late lunch or an early dinner. When the doorbell rang about fifteen minutes later, I figured it was the pizza, and I asked Robert to answer the door while I got the money. Right away, though, I heard a familiar voice.

"I'm in the kitchen, Mary," I called out.

"How nice to see you again," I heard her say sweetly, and then into the kitchen marched my best friend, a highly confused expression on her face. "Would you mind telling me what is going on," she hissed, sounding more like a mother than my mother did.

"Hush," I said.

"Hush nothing," she said, but softly at least. "Bulldozer Boy is in your living room, and it looks like he's planning to stay for a while."

"Robert Sullivan is in my living room, and he's only staying for two days."

"Cath Berry, have you lost your mind?" Her voice started to get louder, and I glared at her.

"He's getting an apartment on Monday, but he

needs a place to stay until then. I want to help him."

"But Cath, how will it look that he's staying with you when your mother's not here?"

Mary's question made me angry, and I had to fight to keep my voice quiet. "I know it's okay, and he knows it's okay. If anyone else doesn't like it, that's *her* problem," I said pointedly.

"Sorry, Cath," Mary said. I don't have a quick temper, so when I snap at her, she knows she's hit a nerve.

"Now we're going to go out into the living room and you're going to be nice to him," I said. I gave her a shove to get her started in the right direction.

Mary sat down primly in the chair, and I perched on the arm of it, within ready elbow reach if necessary. "How nice that you came back to Delaware," Mary said sweetly. "Will you be coming back to school?"

"That's the plan," said Robert, his voice barely carrying, sounding tense.

"Well, we're only five weeks into the first quarter. I'm sure you'll be able to catch up. Will you be a senior?"

"Yes," he answered warily. "I finished my junior year back in Connecticut. I hope I won't be too far behind."

I'd been in his Spanish class for the part of last year that he'd been here, and I knew how smart he was. He'd have no trouble.

I could tell Mary was searching for something to say, which was unusual for her. Normally she can chatter on with anyone about anything. The doorbell donged, and I answered it. This time it was the pizza, and I paid for it and invited Mary to join us. She started to say that she had to be going but I glared at her and she decided she could stay. We gathered around the dining room table, and for a few minutes eating consumed all of our attention. Then, however, the silence started to get awkward. Robert looked even more uncomfortable than Mary, so I figured it was up to me to find a new topic of conversation.

"Mary, I didn't know you were coming over today. What's up?"

"Cath, you wouldn't believe what Mark did last night." Mary glanced briefly at Robert, then launched into a tirade about Mark's latest act of inconsideration. It seemed that he was supposed to take her to the mall at 7:30, but he didn't show up. Then he called at 9:30 and said that he'd been held up, but that he'd be over in a few minutes. Mary had told him to forget it, that the mall was closed and that she'd missed the last day of the sale at The Limited and that it was all his fault. So he had told her that she was a spoiled brat, and she'd told him that he was a thoughtless jerk, and didn't he even care that now she wouldn't be able to buy that sweater that she absolutely adored and had been watching for weeks until it went on sale.

I let Mary go on and on, knowing that eventually she would wind down. I glanced at Robert and saw a smile tugging at the corners of his mouth. I smiled back, then turned my attention back to Mary. Her fights with Mark have been going on for almost two years now, and I'm absolutely used to them. They're always either fighting or making up, and sometimes I don't know which stage I prefer. They've both gone out with others out of spite, but they always end up back together. No wonder I never watch soap operas; Mary provides me with a live version.

Robert seemed content to sit in the living room

while Mary and I cleaned up the few dishes. When Mary left, I walked with her to her car.

"You'd better call me tomorrow and tell me everything," she said as she got ready to leave.

"There won't be anything to tell," I said with a smile.

"Where's he going to sleep?" she asked.

I hadn't thought about that. Somehow it didn't seem right to give him my mother's bed, but it also didn't seem right to give him mine. "The sofa," I said firmly.

"Right, Cath," said Mary with a giggle. "Call me tomorrow."

I turned and walked back to the apartment. It was almost a relief to face the calm that had descended without Mary. Robert was sitting quietly, leafing through one of Mr. Donelly's magazines. He looked up when I came in.

"Mary's really not as crazy as she seems," I said with a smile.

"I can see what good friends you are," he said.

"I don't know what I'd do without her," I said. Then I fell silent. I wondered if Robert had ever had a good friend, a best friend. "Mind if I turn on the news?" I asked. He shook his head, and I grabbed the remote control and pushed the power button. A newscaster's handsome face filled the screen, and his voice filled the silence. We both gave our full attention to him, and gradually we both seemed to relax again. When the news ended, I turned to a movie on HBO. Before it was a third over, I saw that Robert had fallen quietly asleep. I got up and went to the linen closet, pulling out a sheet, blanket, and pillow. I went back to the living room and turned off the television. Robert wakened, looking around tensely.

"It's okay," I said. "If you move for a minute, I'll make you a bed on the sofa."

He got up, then headed toward the bathroom. By the time he returned, I had spread out the sheet and blanket. I guessed it wouldn't be terribly comfortable, but it would have to do. Robert stood awkwardly, looking at me.

"You must be really tired. I hope you sleep well." I turned to walk toward my bedroom.

"Thank you, Cath," he said. That was the first time he'd ever said my name.

"You're welcome," I said. I didn't know what else to say, so I walked to my room, shutting the door behind me.

I stood for a moment, staring at the door, hearing the rustling as he settled in. Sleep tight, I said to him silently. You're going to need every bit of strength you've got if you're going back to school.

Chapter 4

When I woke up the next morning, I curled up contentedly under my quilt, squinting at the clock, which said 7:30. I sighed, pleased beyond belief that it was Sunday and that my mother and Mr. Donelly were in Ireland which meant that I could go back to sleep for as long as my heart desired. Then I suddenly remembered. I wasn't exactly alone. Robert was out there on the living room sofa.

It took me some thought to decide just how I felt about that. On the one hand, I missed the absolute privacy of the last week when I had been living alone. Now don't get me wrong—I love my mother dearly and I like Mr. Donelly and I miss them both, but it was also kind of nice to be my own boss. If I didn't feel like doing the dishes or making my bed or taking out the trash, there was nobody around to make me feel guilty about that. Granted, there was nobody to ask me how my day was or rescue me if there were weird noises in the middle of the night, but on the whole I'd been doing okay on my own.

Still, I kind of liked the thought that Robert was right out there in the living room. I mean, after he disappeared last year, I did some serious thinking about how I could have helped him, been more kind, found out earlier about his father's murder. Now I had the chance to let him see that I was a decent person, that I was willing to help. That's why I had to let him stay here, even though some people might not think it was exactly proper to have a boy staying here without my mother home. I almost giggled. Somehow it seemed like a miracle that Robert talked to me now; in my wildest dreams I couldn't imagine anything beyond that.

Suddenly a new thought hit me. Maybe he had disappeared again. I was assuming that he was out there. What if he had panicked again, taken off in the middle of the night? I listened carefully but heard nothing. Slowly, stealthily, like a kid sneaking a peek on Christmas morning, I sidled out of bed and quietly opened my bedroom door. I looked out into the hallway, then took a few steps toward the living room. At first all I saw was the mound of blanket. Then, however, I saw a tuft of beige, thick hair sticking out. Sure enough, Robert was curled deep within the covers, barely visible but definitely there. I went back to my room with a sigh of relief.

More sleep eluded me, so I tried to figure out what we should do that day. Breakfast, sure, but then what? I knew what I wanted to do, but I wasn't sure that Robert would agree. I wanted to talk, or rather I wanted to listen. I wanted him to tell me what had happened since the day he had left. Still, after years of silence, it seemed like he found it difficult, almost awkward to speak. It wasn't fair to let my curiosity push him faster than he was willing to go. I'd let him decide.

It must have been around 8:30 when I heard him begin to move around. I waited a few more minutes, then put on a pair of jeans, warm socks, and a University of Delaware sweat shirt. When I walked into the living room, he was sitting on the end of the sofa—blanket, sheet, and pillow piled neatly at the other end.

"Good morning," I said brightly. I got no response. "What would you like for breakfast?" This time he seemed to growl softly.

"Not exactly a morning person, are you?" I said. This was a familiar scene to me. I tend to wake up in a pretty good mood, but my mother is barely functional for at least ninety minutes. "Come with me to the kitchen," I said. "You don't have to talk. Just point if you see something that you want for breakfast." Obediently he followed me, and I threw open the pantry, several cupboard doors, and the refrigerator. He wandered from one to the other, finally pointing at a box of cornflakes and a pitcher of orange juice.

"Very good," I said in my best Mr. Rogers voice. "Aren't you being cooperative." Finally I got a hint of a smile from Robert. He perked up considerably after he had swallowed some juice and eaten a big bowl of cereal.

"Thanks," he finally said.

"He speaks," I said sarcastically, then wondered if maybe I shouldn't have joked about such a thing. "What do you want to do today?" I asked quickly.

"I need to go see my aunt," he said after a moment's thought. "The last time I was here I lived with her, and I need to thank her."

"I know," I said. "I went to see her when I was trying to find you."

He looked at me, then went on. "I want her to know that I appreciate what she tried to do for me, but she has kids of her own, and I really think it's better if I live on my own. Dr. Epperson talked to her, though, and she's agreed to serve as a backup

21

if I need help, plus she's going to sign the forms to get me enrolled in school again." His face darkened; we both knew how difficult school would be for him. "I also need to do some shopping," he continued. "I guess I need sheets and stuff for the apartment.

"I'll be glad to go shopping with you if you want the company. The mall opens at noon."

"How about if I go to my aunt's now and then come back here and we'll leave for the mall?"

"Sounds like a good plan," I said. We both cleared the table, and he left with the hint of a smile on his face.

Unfortunately, Robert's mood had gone downhill by the time he returned. His eyes looked tormented, almost like they used to last year. He slumped in the chair, elbows on his knees, chin in his hands. Staring straight ahead, he didn't seem aware that I was in the same room. I was torn between reaching out to him and giving him privacy. Finally I just sat down on the sofa, picking up a magazine that I leafed through, focusing on nothing. It must have been at least ten long, silent minutes before Robert spoke.

"Dr. Epperson says that I have to talk to people, have to communicate so that I don't retreat into silence again. She forgot to tell me how hard it is, though."

I put down the magazine and looked at him, trying to find the right words to help. "Was it rough talking to your aunt?"

"No, she was really nice. She understands that I want to live on my own. You want to know the truth? I think she's relieved I'm not living with her again. She has little kids to deal with, and she doesn't need me to complicate her life again."

"I think it would be different this time," I said.

"I know. At least I'd talk to her. But you have to understand that my mother died when I was really young, and my aunt lost contact with my father and me. She doesn't seem much like family."

I thought maybe I was starting to understand his sadness. "You don't have much of a family left, do you?" I said quietly.

"I've known that since my father was killed, but I guess today I felt it even more."

He seemed to be talking a little more easily now, and I decided to risk a question. "Where did you go when you left here last year?"

At first I thought he wasn't going to answer me, and he turned in the chair so that he was angled even more sharply away from me. Finally, though, I heard his soft, husky voice. "I took a bus back to Connecticut, and stayed with Alan, my father's best friend and tennis doubles partner. I just showed up on his doorstep."

"And he let you stay?"

"For a few weeks. Actually, I wasn't there much."

"Where were you?" I asked.

"I was looking for the person who killed my father." I could hear the anguish in his voice, and I was afraid to ask him any more questions even though I was curious. After a pause, Robert continued, sounding like he was pulling the words out one by one. "The reason I rushed through the halls last year and sat in the back and never talked to anyone is because I couldn't stand anyone behind me, couldn't trust anyone. My father was shot from behind by a murderer the police never caught, and I couldn't even help. I couldn't help the police because I never saw the person, never turned around in time. I couldn't help my father, either. I think that if the police had caught the person who shot my father, I would have been okay. Not great, but okay. When they didn't, though, I stopped trusting in anyone or anything. Cath, my father didn't deserve to die. He was a good man.''

"I'm sure he was," I said quietly.

"I figured that if he could be killed like that, there was no one left to trust. Every footstep behind me could be the next killer, the next one to pull a gun and shoot another innocent person. I could be next, or you, or anyone.''

I needed to fill the silence he left this time. "There *are* good people," I said, wanting to say something better.

"I know that intellectually, but I couldn't make myself trust in that. Maybe my father knew the person who killed him. According to the police, the odds are good that murders are committed by someone the victim knows.''

"So you went to search for your father's killer?''

"Yes," Robert answered. "All day, every day, and far into every night, I walked for miles and miles, hours and hours, through all of Ridgeport. I hung around the tennis courts where my father was killed, walked through stores and streets, searched the faces of everyone I passed. My dad and I were really close. We used to joke that we could read each other's minds. That's why we could play tennis together so well. I always knew where he'd be on the court, where his shots would land, when he'd charge the net, when he'd stay back.''

When I'd been looking for the solutions to the mystery of Robert, I'd searched the newspaper files. Articles had reported the victories of Brendan and Robert Sullivan in father/son tennis tournaments.

"I figured that I would be able to *sense* my father's killer, that the evil would reach me just as it had reached him."

"Weren't you afraid you might be in danger?" I asked.

"I hoped I was," Robert said calmly. "Being killed would have been a relief."

"You never found him," I said, a statement rather than a question. I wondered briefly why I was so sure that Brendan Sullivan's father was killed by a man.

"No," said Robert, "and finally Alan realized that I couldn't keep going like that, barely eating, just walking and searching. So he called Dr. Epperson and she took me back to the hospital where she works."

"You went to school there?"

"I had tutors, and I finished my credit requirements for eleventh grade. Mainly, though, I listened to Dr. Epperson and I thought."

"What did you decide?"

"Dr. Epperson said something that finally cut through to me. She told me that if I didn't start living again, then two people had been killed that night. It was bad enough for my father to have lost his life, but she said I shouldn't give the killer the rest of my life, too. After all, I'd already given him the last two years. She told me that if I had been shot that night instead of my father, that my father would have been very sad and he would have mourned for me, but he would have kept on living and, eventually, trusting and caring."

I was glad that Dr. Epperson had found the right words. "She's right, isn't she?" I asked.

"Yes. I still want my father's killer to be caught. I want to look into that person's eyes and find out why my father died. Still, though, I'm not helping my father or punishing his killer by ruining my own life.''

His words were strong but his voice was sad.

"It's not easy, is it?"

"It's the hardest thing I've ever known in my life. You wouldn't believe how easy it becomes, how safe it feels after a while to not talk, to block everyone out.''

"I'm glad you came back," I said.

"I needed to. I didn't want to stay in Ridgeport, where everything reminds me of my father. I have to finish high school. At first Dr. Epperson and I discussed my going to a different school for my senior year, but it was my decision to come back here. I ran away once, and I have something to prove to myself. I'm not going to spend the rest of my life running.''

So that filled in the missing pieces. Robert had battled his silence and his pain, and he was back. I was glad to have another chance to know him, to understand.

"Enough of this heavy, depressing stuff," Robert said, pulling himself out of the chair. "What's for lunch?"

"What is this? You think I'm your private cook, ready to jump at your command?" It was a relief to be able to joke again.

"You mean you're going to let me starve?"

"I mean let's get started on your shopping and we can get something to eat at the mall.''

"It's a deal," he said with what was actually a smile. As I locked the door behind us, a smile was on my face as well.

Chapter 5

I drove to the mall in the trusty red VW bug that I have virtually inherited from my mother. I mean, it's gotten to the point where she asks my permission if she wants to use it. Robert and I didn't talk much on the way there, but it was okay, not a tense or uneasy silence. The radio was on, and the music filled the car, blending with the tinny rumble of the engine. I parked in the far stretches of the parking lot, not wanting to deal with the parking lot maniac drivers who practically smash into each other in pursuit of the perfect parking spot.

Robert and I walked to the closest entranceway, discussing what he needed to buy. We had decided that sheets and towels were the first necessities, and the signs in the mall advertising Clover Day Sales at Strawbridge and Clothiers sent us in that direction. Robert was certainly easy to shop with; the first sheets without flowers and the first towels without butterflies suited him fine. We headed toward the Food Court, a section of the mall with small tables encircled by all kinds of food stalls. My choice was easy—french fries and a large diet soda. Robert took a little longer before settling on a large roast beef sandwich and a milkshake.

We found a table and started in on the food.

"Tomorrow my aunt and I are going to school to get me registered and scheduled. Then I'll go back to the rental office and see if I can get into the apartment."

"Do you want me to help?" Somehow I was losing my enthusiasm for going back to school. Besides, one day off wouldn't hurt me.

"No, you've done enough. If everything works out, I can get my stuff off your living room floor tomorrow, and you can get back to normal. Then I can start school on Tuesday." There was no great enthusiasm in his voice.

"I know it will be hard, but school will be different this time," I said.

"I don't expect much," Robert said. "If people will just leave me alone, that will be fine."

"You know they'll be curious," I said. "I mean, last year you wouldn't speak at all." And you barrelled through the halls, knocking any number of them down, I mentally added.

"I know," he said. "And they deserve to look at me like I'm some kind of freak. That's part of what I caused for myself, and it's part of what I have to face."

"Sounds like a pretty serious test of character," I said.

"My father taught me never to run away from a challenge," Robert said. "I hope I'm up to this one."

"You are," I said, and I meant it. I just hoped that he believed it.

We finished our lunch and headed back through the mall. Robert saw them before I did, and I could see his face get tense and the pace of his walking quicken.

"What is it?" I asked. Then I followed the direction of his eyes. There, approaching from the opposite direction, was a familiar trio of people—Tony, Cyndee, and Mark. Seeing Mark, I looked around for Mary, since the two of them are usually together, but she wasn't in sight.

I grabbed Robert's arm for a moment, slowing him down. "It's fine," I said. "Consider it practice for school." As the three got closer, I could tell that they had seen us. Cyndee stared blatantly, and Mark glanced appraisingly at Robert, a scowl crossing his face. Only Tony seemed composed, but that was just his way. He was probably as shocked as the others. When we were no more than ten steps apart, Cyndee stepped closer to Tony and linked her arm around his waist, bumping her hip against his.

Until that moment, I had been focusing all of my attention on Robert, worrying about his reaction. Suddenly I became aware of my own feelings. My stomach lurched at the sight of Cyndee, her carefully casual blonde hair now brushing against Tony's shoulder. A voice within me, though, was providing a calming monologue. He has to play his games, the voice said.

"Are you okay?" Robert's voice made me jump. I looked at him in amazement. What did he mean? He was the one I was worried about.

"I'm fine," I said, trying to sound more cheerful than I felt. By this point we were face to face with Tony, Cyndee, and Mark.

"Why look who it is," Cyndee said in a sickeningly sweet voice. Somehow I knew she wasn't referring to me. "I thought you'd left us for good."

Robert stood silently, and for a moment I thought he wasn't going to say anything. I didn't help. I wanted him to answer Cyndee, to show them that this time he would talk. Let that rumor get spread around school tomorrow so people could get used to the idea before Robert appeared. I figured Cyndee would be the perfect one to spread the word. As subtly as I could I elbowed Robert.

"I'm back to finish my senior year," Robert said softly, and then lapsed back into silence. There. It wasn't much, but it would do.

"Tony, did you know that . . . Cath's friend was back?" Cyndee hesitated, searching for a way to identify Robert. I realized that she only remembered him as Bulldozer Boy.

"No," said Tony. He looked slightly uncomfortable through all of this. Mark, on the other hand, was just looking increasingly surly.

"Why Tony, you bad boy. Why didn't you tell me? You know I don't like it when you keep secrets from me," Cyndee said in a little girl voice. I felt like throwing up my french fries.

"You know, Robert, we really better get going. Nice seeing you all." With those words I started walking again, Robert right beside me.

How can Tony stand her, I asked myself. How can he actually hold a conversation with her? I doubt if he likes her for her intellect, and maybe they have other things to do besides talk, I figured. This time I was the one who started walking faster, and Robert was the one who reached out to slow me down.

"Tony gets to you, doesn't he?" he said.

"No," I answered hastily. "That's ancient history."

"Right," Robert said.

"No, really," I protested. "I wish he and Cyndee nothing but happiness."

Robert looked at me skeptically.

"Well, maybe happiness with a mild case of food

poisoning and a few major arguments thrown in," I said with an attempt at a chuckle.

"Seeing them made me think that maybe this was all a bad idea," Robert said. "Maybe I'm not ready to go back to school."

"What can they do to you?" I asked. "They're so caught up in their own lives that they'll lose interest in you. Yes, you'll be a novelty for a while, but if you don't give them ammunition, they'll forget about you."

"And find someone new to pick on?"

"Yes," I said. "I hate to admit it, but you're right. This year there's a guy who has shaved half of his head and wears a safety pin in his nose. He's a pretty hot topic."

"This is sad," Robert answered. "Suddenly I'm grateful to that guy." We both laughed, shoving open the door and leaving behind the recycled mall air for the crispness of the outdoors.

Chapter 6

That evening was calm and comfortable. Robert and I made a stir-fried concoction for dinner and watched another movie on HBO. We didn't talk a lot, but we didn't need to. In a way, I was sad that he was leaving the next day.

He was barely stirring the next morning when I was ready to leave for school. I took my mother's house key off her ring and laid it on the end table.

"Just lock the door behind you," I said.

Robert mumbled something incomprehensible, and I left.

I ran into Mary at my locker before homeroom. "So what happened?" she asked. "Tell me everything, and I mean everything."

"Nothing happened," I replied calmly.

"Cath Berry, don't you dare lie to me. Something must have happened."

"Mary, the most exciting thing we did was go to the mall. Didn't Mark tell you he saw us there?"

"Mark was at the mall? When?" Mary's voice sharpened, and I wished I hadn't said anything.

"Sunday afternoon. Don't worry. He was with Tony and Cyndee."

"Why didn't he invite me along? What a jerk. I

hate him." Mary slammed a fist against my locker, making the metal ring.

I paid very little attention to Mary's outburst. She is one of the most dramatic people I know. Life is a stage to Mary, and she definitely plans to be a star. She either loves or hates Mark, and it varies not only from day to day, but from moment to moment. Still, Mary and I are best friends, and we have been since elementary school.

"Mary, I'm sure there's a good reason why Mark didn't invite you. Maybe he didn't know he was going until the last minute. Maybe he called and you weren't home. Maybe he went to the mall to buy you a present."

I could see Mary's fist unclench. "A present for me? That's right. That's what he was doing."

"It's just a possibility, Mary."

Suddenly Mary's attention shifted. "Cath, you saw Tony with Cyndee? That girl is such a flirt. I can't stand her." The warning bell rang, and we headed off in different directions to homeroom.

It was an uneventful school day, and I found my mind wandering over and over again to Robert. I found myself looking forward to seeing him at the end of the day, and the dismissal bell sent me sprinting for the car. I only stopped long enough for a quick word with Mary.

"I'm going to see how Robert made out today. I'll call you tonight."

"Don't bother."

I was startled by her harsh response. She'd been fine when I talked to her at lunch. She saw the look on my face. "I'm sorry, Cath. I just won't be home."

"A hot date with Mark?" I asked teasingly.

"Not exactly," Mary said, walking away.

I puzzled over her strange mood, but then took off for my car. Eventually Mary would tell me what was on her mind. She always did.

When I got home and unlocked the door, a naked living room floor greeted me. That answered at least one of the questions—Robert must have gotten the apartment. I threw down my books and changed into jeans, a turtleneck, a heavy red cotton sweater, and my favorite Reeboks. Then I walked down through the apartment complex to the building where Robert should now be. I caught up with him just as he was taking the last awkward armful out of his car.

"Let me help," I said, grabbing a backpack off the top of the heap.

"Thanks," he said, stumbling off ahead of me.

"Everything worked out with the lady at the rental office?" I asked.

"Yes, much to her surprise, I could provide people to vouch for me and enough money to ease her fears. I registered at school, too," he said, shoving open the door and throwing everything down on the floor. I added the backpack to the chaos. The apartment looked even worse than I remembered.

"Cath, I have some bad news for you," Robert said. "I'm really sorry for what I did." Robert had thrown himself down on the floor, leaning his head against a box overflowing with books. I stood over him, suddenly apprehensive.

"What did you do?" I asked, my mind racing. Had he gotten in trouble at school already?

"After you left this morning, I went into the kitchen and got some cereal for breakfast." He stopped, and I almost kicked him to get him started again.

"That's no problem," I said. "You're welcome to whatever food was there."

"That's not all," he said, rolling over on his side so that he was curled away from me.

I stepped over his prone body so that once again I could look down on his face.

"What happened next?" I asked, feeling like I was dealing with a four-year-old who had robbed the cookie jar.

"The phone rang," he said.

Still I didn't see a problem. "Good for the phone," I said sarcastically. "It's supposed to ring. It was just doing its job."

"I answered it. Cath, I don't know why I did, but I was standing right next to it and it rang and it startled me so I answered it."

Suddenly I was starting to see the beginning of a problem. "Robert, who was on the phone?"

"Your father."

"My father? You talked to my father? I can't believe you did that. What did you say to him?"

"He asked if this was the Berry residence, and I said yes. He asked if you were home, and I said no. He asked who I was and I said a friend. He told me to tell you to call your father as soon as you got home and he left a number for you and then he hung up." Robert curled up into a ball as soon as he finished his story.

I sank onto the floor beside him and pried his head out of his arms. I put my face close to his and hissed, "You told my father you were a friend who just happened to be there in the apartment when I wasn't even home?"

"I guess so. I didn't exactly mean to, but I was barely awake and I wasn't really thinking and I'm

35

sorry and I know that was a rotten way to repay your hospitality and you can hit me if you want to."

All of his words came spilling out without so much as a breath to interrupt them. "Robert, I'm not going to hit you. I know you didn't mean to get me in trouble, but how the devil am I going to explain this to my father?"

"How about telling him the truth?"

"Now there's a radical thought," I said. "If he left a number, at least he must still be in California. Maybe I could tell him that you were a repairman or something."

"I said I was your friend."

"Great," I said. "Couldn't you be an especially friendly repairman?"

"Cath, your father didn't sound like a stupid man."

"I guess it's going to have to be the truth, then."

"Do you want me to talk to him and try to help explain?" Robert didn't sound very thrilled with that possibility, but at least he offered. He didn't know my father. I knew it wasn't going to be easy convincing my dad that he didn't need to rush home on the next plane to rescue my reputation or something.

"Thanks, but you've done enough talking to him for one day." I looked around the apartment. "This place is a mess. You'd better get to work."

"Doing what?" Robert asked. "Looks fine to me."

"But you need to unpack these boxes and bags, and put things away, and get organized."

"Why? I sort of like the casual look."

I got to my feet and walked out to the kitchen. I opened the refrigerator and saw nothing but the white interior walls and empty shelves. "What's for dinner?" I asked sweetly.

"I haven't gotten to food yet," Robert said. I could hear him thrashing around in the living room.

"If you tell me what you want and give me some money, I'll go to the grocery store while you unpack," I said, feeling noble to be helping someone who had caused such havoc with my father. Actually, I was delaying going home, where I knew I'd have to call him.

"Let's see, I need my cornflakes and milk and some sugar to put on them, and how about some root beer and sour cream potato chips? That should do it."

"What about dinner?"

"Oh yeah. How about some hot dogs and mustard? And hot dog rolls. I'll buy lunch at school. And pickles. I like dill pickles. And orange juice."

"Dill pickles and orange juice? That's disgusting."

"Not together," he said, walking to the kitchen with his wallet in his hand. He gave me a twenty-dollar bill. "Thanks."

I walked home, retrieved the VW, and went to the store. His limited list only took me a few minutes to gather. By the time I got back, he had actually made a good-sized dent in the pile of belongings. I wasn't sure it was an improvement to reveal more of that puke-green carpet. I handed over the groceries, then decided that I had delayed enough. I had to call my father.

I drove the few blocks back, and walked slowly to the door. I was rehearsing my speech in my head as I unlocked the door. Even as I put the key in the lock, I could hear the phone ringing. I moved slowly, willing the phone to stop. I was sure it was

37

my father, and I wasn't quite ready yet. The phone kept ringing and ringing and ringing, and it was a relief when it finally stopped.

I fixed myself a sandwich, watched the news, and did some homework. At nine o'clock, I knew I could wait no longer. With the time difference, it would be six in Los Angeles, and my father had probably left a number at work.

I walked toward the kitchen, steeling myself to face a lecture about my poor judgment. I was almost to the phone when it rang. He beat me to it, I thought.

I answered it, saying hello somberly, ready for my father's angry voice.

"Cath, I need you." Mary's voice sounded strangled, as if the words were being choked out.

"Mary, what's wrong?" I was used to her constant upsets, but this sounded worse than usual. I got no answer. "Is it your grandfather?" I knew he was old and sick. No answer. "Have you been in an accident? Are you sick? Where are you?" No answer. I was starting to panic. I heard a crack as the receiver hit something, a counter or the floor.

"Mary!" I screamed. "Mary! What's going on? Where are you? Answer me. Tell me where you are."

"Cath, is that you?" The voice I heard belonged to Mary's mother.

"Yes," I answered frantically. "What's wrong?"

"Can you come over to the house?" Mary's mother said. "Something terrible has happened to Mark."

Chapter 7

I was out of the house seconds after I hung up the phone, and in a matter of minutes I was at Mary's house. The whole way I chanted to myself to wait and see, not to imagine what could have happened. Still, I was trembling when I got to the front door.

I didn't even have a chance to knock before the door was opened. Mary's mother was in front of me, her eyes red and her face streaked with tears. She put her arms around me and hugged me tightly. I pushed back from her, needing to know what was going on. It was then that Mary appeared, and the sight of her terrified me. She was so pale that her lips looked almost blue, and her normally pretty face was dominated by eyes glassy with tears. I went to her and put my arms around her, stroking her hair.

"Tell me, Mary."

I could feel the sobs shake her body.

"Come on, Mary," I said gently, quietly. "You have to tell me so that I can help."

"The police were just here," she finally said. I could barely make out the words.

"The police?" I asked. "What did they want? Tell me, Mary."

"Mark is dead." She choked on the last word,

and she was shaking so hard that I didn't think she could possibly remain standing. Her mother came over and tried to lead her away from me, but instead Mary just sank to the floor. I sat next to her, my arms around her.

Mary's mother spoke from over us. "The police found Mark's body in a parking lot off Main Street. When they contacted his family, his mother said that he had left a few hours earlier and that he had said he and Mary were going to the library."

"I didn't see Mark," Mary said shakily. Her arms tightened around me. "How could I have been with him when I was with you, Cath?"

I know that Mary felt my body stiffen, and I buried my head against her shoulder so that her mother couldn't see my face. I hadn't even had a chance to deal with the knowledge that a friend, someone Mary loved, was dead, and now Mary was lying to her mother. Why? What was I going to do? I couldn't think straight, couldn't get my mind to digest all of this.

"What happened to Mark?" I asked, biding time, trying to understand.

"The police don't know yet," Mary's mother answered. "They need to do an autopsy, and then they need to talk to Mark's friends."

"Don't say that," Mary screamed. "Don't talk about him like he's some piece of evidence, not Mark. Stop it. Stop it now."

"I'm sorry, honey," Mary's mother said, bending down to touch Mary's hair. Mary flinched away from her. "I wish I could help, but I don't know what to say to you."

"Just leave me alone," Mary cried. "Just leave me alone with Cath."

Mary's mother stood up, and I looked up to meet her eyes. "It's okay," I said. "Let me talk to her."

I got Mary to her feet, and we walked slowly up the steps to her bedroom. She didn't even throw herself on her bed like she usually does; instead, she lowered herself down slowly, gently, as if she were very old and fragile and might break. Once again sobs shook her slender body, and I took her hands and held them.

"Mary, you have to tell me what's going on."

"Cath, Mark can't be dead. He can't be."

"I'm sorry," I said, knowing how useless those words were.

"Even when I was mad at him, I still loved him."

"I know you did." I let her cry, and I cried with her. Eventually, her breathing evened a little.

"Mary, you need to tell me where you were tonight. Were you with Mark?"

"No," she said quickly, sharply, and I believed her.

"Where were you?"

"I was with you."

"No, Mary, you weren't with me. You can tell me the truth. You know that."

"I don't want to talk about it. Don't ask. Not now. Don't ask me anything now." Her voice was starting to rise hysterically, and I stopped talking. She curled up on the bed, and I curled up beside her.

"It's okay," I said to her. "Just cry. You don't have to talk to me." I held onto her until she cried herself into exhaustion, until she was quiet, either from sleep or from shock. I heard her mother come to the doorway, and she walked over and looked down at her daughter. She didn't say a word, but

41

rather shook her head sadly and went back out of the room.

Even in the darkness, I could pick out familiar things in Mary's room—the bulk of the huge bear perched in the rocking chair, the figurines on her bureau, the clutter on her desk. Mary and I had spent a lot of time growing up in this room, and suddenly I would have given anything in the world to go back to the days when the worst crisis we had was that the points were worn down on the crayons or we hadn't finished our book reports or the guy Mary had a crush on in fifth grade liked someone else.

I didn't want Mark to be dead.

And I didn't want Mary to be lying about where she'd been.

Hour after hour I stayed curled on the bed next to the motionless body of my best friend, trying to remember, trying to forget.

Chapter 8

It was just after dawn when I woke, still curled up on Mary's bed. She was breathing deeply and evenly, and I didn't want to disturb her. Still, I knew that if I waited much longer, her mother would be up and undoubtedly would want to know where Mary and I had been the night before. I didn't want to deal with those questions.

As slowly as I could move, inch by inch, I got up. Mary sighed but did not awaken. I went to her desk and in the dim morning light, I found paper and pen.

Mary—
I'll be home. Try to come over so we can talk.
                                        —Cath

I grabbed a piece of tape from the dispenser on her desk and looked around for a place where she was bound to look. Finally I stuck the note on one of the posts at the foot of her bed.

The steps creaked under my feet, and the door came open with a groan. Still, I made it out without disturbing Mary's parents. The sound of the VW's engine echoed in the quiet neighborhood, and I pulled away as quickly as I could. I arrived home only to discover that I didn't want to face the empty apartment. I wanted my mother to be there, maybe even my father.

My father. A surge of panic ripped through me. I hadn't called him back. What must he think by now? Whatever it was, it would have to wait. It was early here, and that made it three hours earlier yet in California, not an ideal time to call. Besides, I hadn't figured out what to tell him. At the moment, I didn't seem to know what to tell anybody.

I put the key in the lock, but I couldn't turn it. I couldn't face the silence. Instead I wheeled around and walked back down to the first floor and out the door. I walked the blocks to Robert's apartment with a slow yet determined trudge. It was only when I faced his door that I hesitated. This was an ungodly hour to visit, but I needed to talk to someone. I knocked on his door, and then, not hearing footsteps, rang the doorbell.

His hair was disheveled, his eyes were squinting in the light, and his sweat pants and T-shirt were rumpled. One look at him reminded me of how much difficulty he seemed to have waking up in the morning, and I almost turned around and ran.

"Good morning," I said softly.

"Morning," I guess he answered, the syllables barely discernible.

"I need to talk to you," I said. "I know it's early, but it's important."

"I hope so," he said, his voice a grumpy growl.

"Never mind," I said. "Forget it. This was a bad idea. I'm sorry." I turned to walk away, filled with regret over my impulsiveness.

"You come right back here," Robert said. I looked back to see him rubbing his eyes and running his hands through his thick hair. "I'm awake now."

He didn't look like it, but I figured he'd be even more angry if I woke him up and left than if I woke him up and at least explained why. I walked in and threw myself down on the sofa. He sat cross-legged on the floor and looked up at me.

"Robert, do you remember Mark?" That was a pretty stupid question. Mark had been one of those who had tormented Robert the worst last year.

"Of course I do."

"He was killed last night."

Robert's eyes opened fully, and he gazed at me in confusion. "Killed? How?"

"We're not sure yet. His body was found in a parking lot off Main Street last night."

"How did you find out?"

"Mary. Mark was her boyfriend."

"Was she with him? Did she see what happened?" Robert's voice sharpened, intensified.

"No, she wasn't there. As a matter of fact, I don't know where she was." I told Robert about Mary's lie, and about my inability to get her to tell me the truth about last night. I was worried that I was violating Mary's confidence by talking about it, but I had to tell someone. I had to figure out what to do. I could feel the tears coming back to the surface, and I could also feel panic growing inside of me. I hated the thoughts that were growing in my mind, thoughts that had my best friend somehow involved in Mark's death. That couldn't be. It just couldn't.

"Are you okay?" Robert asked softly. He was studying my face.

"I'm sure not great," I said shakily.

Robert got up off the floor and came to sit on the sofa beside me. He reached out a hand, but then withdrew it before he touched me. I understood, remembering how hard it was for him to involve himself with anyone, knowing that this must be bringing back painful memories for him. "I hate to ask you this, but do you think Mary might be involved?" He saw instant anger flash in my eyes, and he spoke again before I could. "I know she's your best friend, and I'm not saying she did anything on purpose, but could she have been involved accidentally?"

My anger died as quickly as it had been born, because even though I hated hearing my own fears put into words, I knew they were a possibility. "I don't think so," I said after a moment's thought. "Mary is emotional and she's always creating scenes, but she's not violent, and she would never intentionally hurt someone."

"Accidentally?" Robert asked.

The tears that had been threatening now spilled down my face. Mark was dead, and my best friend was probably a suspect. How much worse was this going to get?

"I didn't mean to upset you even more," Robert said. "I'm sorry. Forget I asked that."

"I can't forget it," I said. "I just have to get some answers from Mary. I'd better go home in case she comes over."

"The police will probably want to talk to her," Robert said, and once again I suspected he was speaking from experience.

"If she tells them she was with me, they'll want to talk to me, too. What am I going to do?"

"I think you know the answer to that." His voice was certain, and I looked at him, met his calm eyes.

"I guess I do," I said.

I left for home, the tears drying on my face as I walked.

Chapter 9

As soon as I got home, I called my father in California. I knew that the ringing of the phone would make him imagine the worst, but he probably already was imagining pretty bad things, so I might as well fill him in. Besides, this did not have the makings of a good day, and I figured I should face one problem before the next one arrived.

"Dad, it's me. I'm sorry to wake you up, but I wanted to talk to you."

"Cath? Just what is going on?" I could hear sleep and confusion in my father's voice, with anger surfacing quickly.

"Dad, there's been an accident."

"Are you okay? My God, Cath, what's . . ."

I cut him off before he could panic any further. "I'm fine, Dad. It's Mark, Mary's boyfriend. He was killed last night."

"Was he drinking and driving?"

I was angry that my father automatically assumed that Mark was at fault. "No," I snapped. "He wasn't."

My father must have heard the anger. "I'm sorry, honey. It sounds like I'd better get home and help you deal with all of this."

"No, Dad, please don't. Everything's under control."

"It certainly doesn't sound like it."

I had to admit that he had a point there, but having my father home would give me more to deal with, not less. "Dad, all I can do is help Mary get through this, and there's no way you can help with that."

"Cath, this office is in chaos, but if you need me, you just say the word and I'll be on the next plane."

How could I stay angry with him? He was often difficult to deal with, but I knew he loved me. It was just that he had been gone for years after the divorce. In all honesty, he simply didn't know me very well. "Thanks. I appreciate the offer, and if I need you, I'll call."

"Do you promise?"

"Yes, I do. Try to go back to sleep now."

"Cath, who answered the phone . . ."

I pretended I didn't hear the question. "Bye, Dad. I'll talk to you soon." With that I hung up, then stood frozen by the phone, waiting to see if he would call back to pursue his question. When two minutes had passed without a call, I figured I was temporarily safe. I went to my bedroom and curled up under my quilt, exhausted yet wide awake.

I wasn't sure how much time had passed before I heard the doorbell. A glance at the clock beside my bed told me it was seven o'clock. I hurled my body off the bed and rushed to the door, certain I knew who was there. I was right.

Mary still looked terrible. Dark shadows hollowed her eyes, and she was frighteningly pale. "Come in," I said, reaching for her arm, pulling her forward. Mechanically she walked with me to the sofa and sat down. "Do you want something to drink? Orange juice? Hot chocolate?"

"No," Mary said hollowly.

"Mary, I'm so sorry. What can I do to help?"

"Tell the police I was with you last night." There was a pleading tone in her voice, and I dreaded what I had to do next.

"I can't lie to the police, Mary."

"You're not my friend, then." Her voice got louder, harsher, more panic-filled.

"Mary, you know I'm your friend. It's just that you're asking me to do something that's wrong. Besides, it won't work. The police will figure it out. Just tell them the truth, Mary. Tell *me* the truth."

"No," Mary said, starting to breathe rapidly. I could see her hands shake as she twisted them together. "Just this one lie, Cath, no more, I promise. Just say we were at the library, or went to McDonalds, anything. Just this once. Please, Cath. Just this once."

"Mary, you're not thinking clearly. It would be easy for the police to double-check at the library or McDonalds or anywhere else. If they find out you're lying, then you *are* going to be in trouble." Mary was becoming more and more agitated, and part of me wanted to tell her that I would lie, that I would do anything to help her. Another part knew, though, that lies wouldn't work, not when a person's death was involved.

"I have to go." Mary rose quickly, and was headed for the door when the phone rang. We both froze.

"Don't answer it," Mary said sharply.

"I have to. It's probably my father." I went to the phone, dreading the voice I would hear. Instead, I heard Mary's mother.

49

"Cath, is Mary there?"

"Yes, she is." Mary came up beside me, frantically shaking her head no.

"Tell her that she needs to come home. The police want to see her at the station. Her father and I are waiting to take her."

"Would it be all right if I came, too?" I asked. I didn't like the way Mary was looking at me.

"Thank you, but I don't think so. They just need to ask Mary some questions about last night. Please tell Mary we need to leave right away." With that, she hung up.

"Mary, your parents are waiting to take you to the station. The police need to ask you some questions."

"I won't go." For the first time, a flush of color rose in her cheeks.

"You have to." I tried to put as much calm into those words as I could.

"No I don't. They can't make me."

"Mary, I think they can. Just answer their questions and tell the truth."

"I don't want to."

"Mary, I really don't think that matters right now. Don't you want to help them catch the person responsible?" I stopped before I had to say "for Mark's death."

"It won't change anything."

"No, but it will put some questions to rest." All I could think of was Robert and what he had suffered by not knowing who his father's killer was. "Mary, answer the questions. Tell them the truth."

"You make it sound simple," Mary said softly.

"It's more simple than lying," I said, trying not to sound like some kind of saint. "Mary, I know you didn't have anything to do with Mark's death."

Silence greeted my words. I looked at Mary, but she was not meeting my eyes. I stopped, thought hard, but then said what had been twisting in my mind since last night. "Did you?"

Mary's head jerked up, and her eyes bored into mine. "How could you ask that? How could you be my friend and ask me that?" She whirled around and ran for the door. I wanted to stop her, but I knew I couldn't.

I knew I shouldn't have said that; I could only imagine how Mary must be feeling. She must think I was betraying all of our years of friendship.

Still, her behavior was making certain questions inevitable. She couldn't possibly be involved in Mark's death.

Could she?

Chapter 10

I couldn't face school. There was simply no way that I could deal with it—with trying to act like nothing was wrong, with answering questions about Mary, with hearing rumors about Mark. Instead, I paced around the apartment, going from room to room, not sure of what I was looking for, finding nothing. My mind agonized with Mary, wondering what the police were asking her, fearful of what she might be saying.

When the doorbell donged, I was too tired and worried to even jump at the sound. I opened the apartment door without looking out the peephole first; I figured it would be the police. Instead, it was Tony.

I thought I was under control, but as soon as I saw his face I started to cry. Seeing him was just more than I could deal with. I put my hands up to hide my tears, trying uselessly to regain my composure. I heard the door shut, and then Tony's arms were around me and I held on to him and he hugged me tightly against him. I cried for Mark, for Mary, for myself. I cried for how much could be lost without warning, without time to say what you meant to say. I think I even cried for Tony, for what used to be between us, for what we had lost and the sadness of it. I started to get scared that I would never stop crying, scared that by the time the tears stopped there would be nothing left inside of me.

My face was burrowed into Tony's neck, and eventually I came to realize that all the tears were not my own. I lifted my face to look at him, and his face was wet. I hid my head again, unable to face his pain on top of my own.

It seemed like hours passed, but it couldn't have been that long. Finally my crying exhausted itself, and I clung silently to Tony, barely able to stand. "I'm sorry," I finally whispered. "You must think . . ."

"Hush," he said, rubbing my back. "You don't have to say a word." His kindness made me cry again, but this time the tears ended faster. He must have felt the trembling in my legs because he led me to the sofa. I curled up beside him, turned so that I could still bury my face in his shoulder. His hands rubbed my back, then held me tight.

Finally I heard his voice, hardly more than a whisper. "I can't believe he's dead. I saw him that same day, full of laughter and plans. It's not fair. He was too young to die."

"I know," I replied. "It seems like only old people should die, people who are sick and worn out and have lived their lives. Not someone who's only seventeen. Not Mark." Then I gave voice to the question that was beginning to nag at me more and more. "What happened to him?"

"What do you know?" Tony asked, and his voice sounded almost suspicious.

"Only that he was found in a parking lot off Main Street."

"That's all I know, too." Something in Tony's

voice worried me. I raised my head to look at him, and he looked away. Stop it, I lectured myself silently. You're getting paranoid. First Mary, now Tony. You have to trust someone.

Don't you?

I curled back up, not wanting to look at Tony, not wanting to see anything. This time it was the telephone that interrupted the silence.

"Don't answer it," Tony said, holding onto me more tightly. "The way things are going, it's probably bad news."

I should have listened to him.

"This is Detective Martin of the police department. May I speak to Miss Catherine Berry?"

Great. What had Mary done? What had she told them? "Speaking."

"I have some questions I'd like to ask you concerning Mark Strassiter. Would it be possible for you to come down to the station?"

"When?" I asked, as if that made any difference.

"I'd prefer right now."

"I'll be there," I said.

"Thank you. Tell the officer at the desk to send you directly in to me."

I hung up, and then went back to stand in front of Tony. "I have to go to the police station," I said dully.

"Why?" Tony asked. "What did you have to do with Mark?"

Now who was suspicious? "Nothing," I snapped. "The detective probably wants to talk to me because I'm Mary's friend."

"Why would that matter?"

The last thing I needed was to get into an argument with Tony. "I'd better go. He's waiting for me." I headed for my bedroom where I considered putting on a dress, but I simply couldn't put forth that much effort. I threw on a pair of navy corduroy pants and a heavy Irish-knit sweater. One look at my face told me that there was no helping my swollen, red eyes, so I brushed my hair and went back out. Somehow I didn't think the detective cared about my appearance.

"I'm sorry, Catherine. I didn't mean to question you." Tony was standing near the door.

"I guess I'd better get used to it," I said.

"Still, you don't need me doubting you. I know you'd never harm anyone, at least not intentionally."

Was he implying that I had accidentally helped kill Mark? This was ridiculous. "I have to go."

"I'll drive you."

"No. Thanks, but I'd better go on my own."

"Are you sure you're okay? You worry me." Tony reached out to rub my shoulder.

"I'll be fine," I said convincingly. I only wished I could convince myself.

I needed to talk to Mary, but I was afraid to. My mind was in a fog, and it felt like it would take far too much energy to find Mary and work out a plausible lie. Still, Mary was my best friend. She would lie for me; I knew that beyond any doubt. Why was it so difficult for me?

The officer at the desk escorted me to a tiny office, and the man who greeted me there was tall, at least 6'2", with bright red hair. His appearance startled me. I guess I've watched too many movies, because I figured detectives went undercover all the time, infiltrating all kinds of groups, blending in with the drug dealers or the Mafia lords or whatever. This man bore a passing resemblance to Bozo the

Clown and wouldn't blend in with any group I could think of.

"May I call you Cathy?" Detective Martin asked.

"It's Cath," I said. Or Catherine if you're Tony, I thought, my mind drifting. Angrily I yanked it back to the present. This was important; I needed to concentrate.

"I'm trying to gain some insight into Mark Strassiter, learn about his friends, his activities, anything that might help us to explain his death."

"You don't think it was an accident?" After all, if it was simply an accident the police wouldn't do all of this, would they?

"Let's just say that we're not sure right now. I'm hoping you can help."

"Why me?"

"I understand that you are a very good friend of . . ." He paused and riffled through some papers on his desk. "Here it is. Mary, who was Mark's girlfriend. She indicated that you and Mark were also friends."

Great. What else had Mary indicated? "Yes, I knew Mark, but I'm much closer to Mary."

"What can you tell me about the relationship between Mark and Mary?"

"They've been dating for over two years now. They argue a lot, but they're really very close."

"They argue a lot?" The detective jumped on that. I was so used to Mary and Mark's arguments that I hadn't really thought about how it would sound to someone else.

"Yes, but nothing serious. I mean, they make up the next day."

"To your knowledge, had they been arguing recently?"

Now how was I supposed to answer that? Was

Mary really mad that Mark had been at the mall with Tony and Cyndee without her? "No more than usual," I said cautiously. "There weren't any serious problems that I know of, and with Mary I'd probably know."

"I see," Detective Martin said, and I was afraid that I heard skepticism in his voice. I decided that I needed more information. Most of all, I needed to know what Mary had told him.

"Look, maybe I could help more if I knew more about what happened."

Detective Martin looked at me searchingly, but then he sighed and leaned back in his chair. "I may as well tell you what we know. It will be in tonight's paper, anyway. It seems that Mark was in the parking lot behind Duffy's Tavern sometime around eight o'clock on Monday night. From all indications he was in a car. A man who was working in the kitchen at the back of the tavern heard a voice yelling something like 'Get out of my car.' He didn't think anything of it; people argue in the parking lot all the time. A car door slammed, and then he thinks a car left. It was a time of night when many cars were coming and going. About five minutes later he heard screaming. A group of University of Delaware students were cutting through the parking lot to get to Main Street and they found Mark's body. The cook ran out, then called for an ambulance. By the time it arrived, Mark was already dead. From all appearances, he had been run over and died from massive internal injuries."

There. Now I had heard all the words. Mark's death was now summarized into a police report. My stomach churned. I felt like crying, but there didn't seem to be any more tears left.

"I'm sorry to have to tell you this." Detective Martin's voice was still professional, emotionless.

"I'd rather know. After all, the rumors at school will be amazing."

"Speaking of school, do you know of anyone who might have reason to dislike Mark? Anyone he argued with? A girl he might have broken up with?"

Great. The person with the biggest grudge against Mark was probably Robert, and I wasn't going to bring that up. No way. "I sure can't think of anyone who would want him dead," I said.

"What about his activities?" Detective Martin pursued. "Have you ever known him to drink or use drugs?"

"Drugs? No way," I said firmly. Mary wouldn't put up with that. "I've known him to drink a little, but not much." One night he and Mary and Tony and I had shared a six-pack of beer in the park, but I didn't want to go into that, either. Suddenly there seemed to be a lot of things I didn't want to go into.

"Anything at all that you can think of that might help us?"

"No," I said. I wanted out of his office, away from his questions.

"One last question," said Detective Martin. I relaxed. Good. I could leave soon. "Where were you on Monday night around eight P.M.?"

I stared at him in amazement. How dare he ask me that? What had I ever done to deserve being asked that? Suddenly my anger turned to fear. What had Mary said? Had she said that she was with me? What should I say? Maybe I should refuse to answer. Did I have to answer? If I didn't, though, I would look like I had something to hide, and I didn't.

"I was home studying," I said. "I came home

from a friend's apartment at about six o'clock, and I was waiting until nine o'clock to call my father."

"Did you call your father?"

"No, not until the next day."

"Was anyone else at home?"

I really didn't want to explain about Mom and Mr. Donelly. "No."

"So there is no way to verify your presence there?"

"No," I said, anger flaring again. "Is that a problem?"

"Not at all, Miss Berry," the detective said. Suddenly he didn't seem to want to call me Cath. "I appreciate your time. If I have any more questions, I'll be in touch."

I just bet you will be, I thought as I walked out. By the time I got to the VW, I was shaking. I couldn't figure out why—fear, exhaustion, sorrow, take your pick. I drove home in silence, not wanting to hear the cheerful voice of some disc jockey introducing the latest hits.

Chapter 11

I tried to talk to Mary later that day, but her mother said that their family doctor had finally sedated her. All her mother would say was that Mary was hysterical after she came out of the police station. That sure created more questions than it answered. The only other thing Mary's mom told me was that Mark's parents had decided on a private memorial service and burial on Friday. They were going to limit it to family and a few close friends, afraid that if hordes of kids showed up, it might turn into some kind of spectacle. They had invited Mary, but her mother wasn't sure if she'd go or not.

I went to bed early, not sure if I could sleep but wanting to escape into a state where I wouldn't have to think anymore. I laid there restlessly, my mind plagued by questions. Where had Mary been the night Mark died? Why had Tony seemed so suspicious? Whose car had Mark been in? What kind of person could have hit him and then just left him there to die? Mercifully, I finally fell asleep, and my dream-tossed sleep was still better than my waking nightmares.

The next morning I woke up at 6:00, and debated what to do next. Finally I decided to go to school.

After all, it would fill the time, and maybe it would distract me a little. It didn't sound like I'd be able to see Mary anyway, and besides, I felt bad about Robert. I didn't know if he'd gone to school yesterday or not, but either way he was bound to be there today, and he could undoubtedly use some moral support.

I put on a pair of baggy jeans and a pale pink oversized sweater. Socks, sneakers, and I was ready. Somehow it didn't seem to matter how I looked. I wasn't hungry, and nothing in the fridge appealed to me, so I grabbed an orange and threw it in my pocketbook. I still had some time left before I needed to leave, so I glanced through my books, trying to figure out what I had missed yesterday. Somehow that didn't matter, either, and I found myself staring at pages but registering nothing. It was almost a relief when it was time to leave.

The first thing I did after I got to school was look for Robert. I thought I knew which homeroom he should be in, but he wasn't there. I headed toward the library, thinking he might be there trying to avoid the masses of people in the hallway, but I was intercepted by a group of girls.

"Cath, have you heard about Mark? Oh, of course you have because of Mary. How is poor Mary? Is she here today? What happened? I heard his skull was smashed. Have you seen the body?" Their voices merged into one, and their questions came too fast to manage. They hovered closer and closer until I was in the middle of a circle of curious eyes and pounding questions. They reminded me of vultures.

"Mary won't be here today." That was the question I chose to answer, and it was probably the one they cared the least about.

"Oh, it's just so terrible," one of the vultures said. With that she gave a dramatic moan and began to cry. The others now circled around her, their arms surrounding her. Within moments, they were all crying. I looked at them in amazement, and then walked away. I had spent a lot of time around Mark and Mary, and I had never seen any of these girls. They might have been acquaintances, but they certainly weren't close friends. I was suddenly very glad that Mary wasn't here to witness this.

I went to homeroom, walking quickly and trying to avoid the questions hurled at me from various people. I was known as Mary's friend, not as me, and suddenly I was a potential source of gruesome tidbits of information about Mark. I had to fight to keep heading for homeroom; what I really wanted was to walk out the door and keep right on walking.

The day got no better. Everywhere I was bombarded by questions I either didn't want to answer or didn't know the answers to. Even worse were all the rumors. Every person seemed to have a new theory about Mark's death, each theory more bizarre than the one before. To add to my misery, I couldn't find Robert. It wasn't until fourth period Spanish class that I finally found him. He was already there when I got to class, slowed down of course by questions, and I had only a moment to talk to him before class started.

"How are you doing?" I asked, stopping by his desk.

There was a long moment's silence, and I was afraid that he had stopped talking again. After this day, I could more fully understand the simplicity of not saying a word. Finally, though, he answered me. "Okay, in a sad kind of way."

"Why sad?" I asked.

"Most people are so busy talking about Mark that they don't have time to worry about me."

He was right. It was sad, too sad for me to be able to think that at least Mark's death had brought a tiny bit of good for someone else.

"Do you have lunch next?" I asked.

"Yes," he answered as the bell rang for class.

"Wait for me," I said, then turned to head for my seat. Robert had been famous for his quick exits from classes last year, and I wanted to be sure I didn't miss him this time.

I don't remember much about class, something about irregular subjunctive verb endings, I think. When class ended, I grabbed my books, relieved to see Robert still seated. We walked out together, and without even saying anything, both of us headed in the opposite direction from the cafeteria. There was no way on the face of the earth that I could deal with that mass of humanity, and Robert must have felt the same way. We headed for the parking lot, and I didn't even look for teachers as we broke the rule about leaving the building during lunch. I settled into the VW, reaching across to unlock the other door for Robert.

The silence between us stretched, but it was a relief, not a source of tension. Finally I reached into my pocketbook and got out the orange, peeling it and then pulling it in half. I held out half to Robert, and he took it silently. The burst of tart juice in my mouth tasted true and honest and real, which was more than I could say for the people in the school. I knew I was being overly harsh, but I couldn't help it.

"I don't think Mary is going to be able to stand school," I finally said into the silence.

"I know what you mean," Robert said. "It's not an easy place."

Suddenly I realized that Mary was not the only one with major adjustments to make. "Are you sure you're okay?" I asked.

"I'm okay," he said, although not with much conviction. "I've heard murmurs of Bulldozer Boy everywhere I've gone, but I had steeled myself for that."

"How could they?" I asked in outrage. "Don't they know your name?"

"Probably not," Robert answered. "Look, Cath, it's okay. I knew when I decided to come back here that I had quite a reputation to live down, but that's part of not running away. It will get better."

"You bet it will," I said fiercely.

"Cath, stay out of it. This is my battle, not yours."

I was surprised at Robert's response, at how quickly he had read my mood. He was right. The mood I was in, I would have loved to punch out the first person who insulted him. What was happening to me? I had never exactly been the brawling type. Suddenly I started to laugh. I was as surprised as Robert was.

"What?" he asked, looking at me with his head cocked in puzzlement.

"How would I ever explain to my mother that while she was in Ireland I was suspended for fighting?"

"I can see the headlines now," Robert answered, laughing also. 'Model Daughter and Student Suspended for Blow Struck for Bulldozer Boy's Honor.' "

" 'Boy May Be Lost Son of Elvis Presley and his Secret Mechanical Mistress,' " I continued, laughing harder now. Suddenly I stopped. What was I doing laughing? Mark was dead, Mary was hysterical, and I was laughing. "I feel guilty," I said to Robert.

"I know what you mean," he said. "Still, we're not doing anybody any good by sitting around being sad. I learned that from Dr. Epperson. It didn't help my father, and it won't help Mark."

He was right. I didn't feel like laughing anymore, but I also didn't feel guilty. "I don't want to go back to school," I said, looking at my watch. There were only two more minutes before the next period started.

"Are you going to let those kids run you out?" Robert asked.

"Yes," I said.

"Wrong," he answered. "Let's go."

I was used to always being the good influence. It was a relief to have someone else take over the job. Obediently I grabbed my books, shoved the orange peels into the glove compartment for lack of a better place, and walked with Robert back into school.

Was it only my imagination that the door shutting behind us echoed like the clang of prison bars?

You know, sometimes I don't think that being a good kid pays off. If there were any justice in the world, I would have been rewarded for going back to school rather than leaving, but no. I made it through fifth and sixth periods, and was heading for seventh, relieved that it was the last period of the day. There, heading down the hallway toward me were Tony and Cyndee. Okay, I said to myself. I can deal with this. I understand Tony now. Even though he was wonderful to me yesterday, that didn't mean that he wasn't going to continue playing his games. Let him.

As our paths approached, I was ready to just say

hello to both of them and keep going. It was Cyndee who had other plans. First she grabbed my arm to stop me. Then she stared at me with large, tear-filled eyes. "How can you stand it?" she asked in a tiny whisper. "I wouldn't be able to stand being in school if I didn't have Tony here to help me." With that, she threw her arms around Tony's neck and began to sob.

Great, I thought. Just what I need. Tony's shoulder must barely have had a chance to dry out from me, and now he has another female wetting it down. Tony was patting Cyndee on the back as if she were a baby that needed burping. He met my eyes over Cyndee's shoulder, and I thought I detected a note of pleading. I shook my head slightly and walked away to class.

The dismissal bell never sounded sweeter. As I headed for my car, storm clouds were rolling in, and the air felt ten degrees colder than it had at noon. Somehow that seemed appropriate.

Chapter 12

It was about 7:00 that night when Mary appeared at my door. I had been trying to get caught up on some homework, but I couldn't concentrate, so Mary centainly wasn't interrupting anything worthwhile. She still looked pale and subdued as she came in and sat down on the sofa, but at least she seemed a little more composed.

"I had to get out of the house," she said. "I love my parents, but it feels like they're smothering me."

"They're just worried about you. So am I," I added.

"Why? I'm not the one who's dead."

"No, but you're one of the ones who is suffering right now."

"Cath, I wish I were dead, too." Mary said the words with no emotion in her flat, toneless voice.

"Mary, I'm sure you do right now. But this will pass. It will get easier."

I almost welcomed the anger with which she responded. "What do you think I'm going to do, just forget about Mark and find a new boyfriend? Well, I won't."

"That's not what I meant, Mary. Of course I don't expect you to forget about Mark, but I also know that you have to go on living. Give yourself time to heal.''

I don't think Mary believed me, but at least she didn't yell—or cry. I know Mary better than I know anyone else on earth except maybe my mother, and I know that she is a survivor. At heart she is a happy person, and that part of her fights against anything that tries to bring her down. It would take some time, but Mary would be fine. The only problem was that I knew that and Mary didn't.

"Cath, who was Mark with?" She paused, then turned so that she was looking straight at me. "He wasn't with me."

I was glad to hear her say that, even though I wish it hadn't been necessary. I still didn't know where *she* had been that night, but at least this helped. "I don't know," I answered, wishing I could help, yet not knowing what to say.

"What are the kids at school saying?"

"Mary, you really don't want to know," I said, remembering all that I had heard.

"Yes I do," she said. "Maybe there's something in it that will help explain this."

I thought about it for a moment, totally undecided. It was bound to upset Mary to hear all of the rumors, yet it was inevitable that she would hear them soon, anyway. After all, eventually she had to come back to school. I decided to trust in the strength that I was convinced resided inside of Mary.

"Okay," I said, "but there are about seventeen versions, and those are only the ones I heard. Are you sure you're ready for this? Maybe we should talk about this in a day or two, when you've had more time to . . ."

"More time to what, Cath?" My silence told her that I didn't want to answer that. "Come on, Cath.

Somewhere there has to be a clue to who Mark was with, and to who killed him." She choked on the words, but she got them out.

"Okay," I said. "Let's make a list."

Mary actually laughed at that. "Cath Berry, that is your answer to life. Write everything down in a list."

Mary had me there. I fill pages and pages with lists—things I need to do, goals for summer vacation, New Year's resolutions, lists for every occasion. Somehow, once I write things down, they become more manageable for me. I also love the satisfaction of crossing off things that I've finished. Still, this would be a list like no other I had ever written—or wanted to write.

I got a sheet of unlined paper plus a couple of magazines to lean on. Then I curled up on the sofa next to Mary, pen poised.

"Do you promise you'll tell me to stop if this gets too upsetting?"

"Just write, Cath," said Mary. She was steadily becoming more like herself. I just hoped this list didn't send her back into hysteria.

"Okay," I said. At the top of the paper I wrote:

RUMORS CONCERNING MARK

It wasn't a great title, but one of the rules of list-making is that each list must have a heading. I thought briefly, then decided that I might as well get the worst one out of the way first rather than working up to it. Mary read over my shoulder as I wrote.

1. Mary did it. She killed Mark because she:
    a. found out he wanted to date another girl

b. found him in bed with another girl
c. is pregnant with his child and he wouldn't marry her

Mary stared at me in amazement. "Is this some kind of sick joke, Cath? Have people really been saying these things?"

"Mary, we're talking rumors here. You know how it works, the more outrageous the better."

"I might be mad at Mark over those, I might even consider killing myself over one of them, but I'd never kill *him*."

"I know that, Mary. So do the people at school, if they'd stop to think it through. They're not thinking; they're just throwing words around to create some excitement. They remind me of some gruesome kind of journalist, each one trying to be the first to get the inside scoop."

"This sure doesn't make me want to go back to school."

"At least it will give you a chance to set them straight." Knowing Mary, she'd do just that.

Wanting to change the topic, I started writing again.

2. Mark was a drug user and/or dealer, and he was killed when a deal went bad. Mark was using or dealing the following drugs:
   a. marijuana
   b. cocaine
   c. crack
   d. speed
   e. angel dust
   f. heroin
   g. LSD

Mary looked at me with even greater amazement than number one had caused. "Cath, if he'd been using all of these drugs, he would have been dead long ago. He didn't use drugs at all, and certainly not all of those. Besides, I know he didn't deal drugs because he was always broke. The last time we went to the movies I had to pay."

I studied her carefully. At least she was getting angry rather than sad.

"Ready for the next one?" I asked. Mary nodded, so I resumed writing.

3. Mark's last name really isn't Strassiter. Instead, it's Strassitori, and his father is in the Mafia. Mark was killed either:
   a. because he had recently become active in the Mafia himself and he was killed by:
      1. a rival Mafia family
      2. the FBI
   b. because his father had displeased some godfather and Mark was killed to punish his father

At least this time Mary actually laughed. "Cath, admit that you're making this up."

"I have a good imagination, but not that good."

"Mark's mother is Polish and his father is German," Mary said. "His father works for Chrysler. That doesn't exactly sound like a Mafia connection to me. Go ahead, Cath. I can't even imagine what's next."

I knew she wouldn't like this one either, but I wrote anyway.

4. Mark was drinking straight whiskey at Duffy's Tavern, and he got so drunk that he passed out in the parking lot and was run over.

"Cath, I've never known Mark to drink anything other than an occasional beer. Besides, he was only seventeen. He couldn't get served."

"Minor details, Mary. Rumors can't be bothered with such little points. Wait until you see the next one." That had her anxiously peering over my shoulder as I wrote.

5. Mark was actually a narc, working undercover for the police department. In fact, he wasn't even really a high school student; he was anywhere from 22 to 27, and his job was to gain the trust of the kids at school and then turn them in for anything from underage drinking to drugs to illicit sex. Someone found out, set up a meeting in the parking lot, and killed Mark. Supposedly several guys who were busted last month for possession now swear that Mark was the one who set them up.

This one left Mary sputtering. "Cath, half of the kids in the school have known Mark since elementary school. How could he be twenty-seven?"

"I guess the police picked him very early and have been grooming him for this role since infancy," I said laughingly as I continued writing. "Wait till you hear this last one."

6. Mark was attacked by a crazed killer who has already killed two boys in Philadelphia and three in Baltimore. The killer only chooses boys who have brown hair and blue eyes, and

he chops their heads off and writes obscene messages with their blood. He is thought to be a devil worshipper following orders given to him by a large orange cat named Psychokitty that hisses in his ear while he sleeps.

"Psychokitty?" Mary asked. "This is sad. Please tell me that there aren't any rumors worse than that."

"That's all I heard," I said, looking over the list. "Do you see anything helpful here?"

"Not exactly," Mary said.

"Did Mark tell his parents where he was going?" I asked on a more serious note.

"He told them that he was going out with me."

"Did you have plans to see him?"

"No," Mary said.

"Did he take his parents' car? Have the police looked for it?"

"No. His parents said that a car pulled up in front of the house, and Mark went out. They didn't even bother to look since they figured it was me."

"Then he must have had plans of some kind. He didn't just leave on the spur of the moment."

"Cath, I want to know who he was with." I didn't like the edge that was building in Mary's voice again.

"I know," I said. "Did you tell the police about this?"

"Yes," she said. "Detective Martin said that he would check with the neighbors to see if anyone saw what kind of car Mark left in."

Suddenly I realized that Mary didn't know that I had been called down to the police station. I didn't want to tell her, but I needed her to know. "Mary,

Detective Martin called and I had to go talk to him."

"What?" she said, her body stiffening. "Why you?"

"I don't know," I said, hoping she would explain. Silence followed. "He asked me where I was on Monday night."

"What did you tell him?" Mary asked.

"I told him that I was home studying," I said, watching for her reaction. "I told him the truth."

"I knew you would," Mary said, and I couldn't decide if there was scorn or respect in her voice.

"Is that a problem?" I asked, desperately wanting to know what Mary had told the detective.

"I hope not," was all she said. "I need to go home now," she said abruptly. "I promised my parents I'd be home early." Before I could say anything more, she was gone.

I sat on the sofa, staring at the door Mary had closed behind her. I wasn't sure if I felt better or worse. I was glad that Mary was functional again, even showing flashes of her old spirit. Still, it upset me that she wasn't fully leveling with me.

We'd never kept secrets from each other, starting from when we were little kids. In fact, it had always seemed impossible for Mary to keep anything from me. Every year she told me what my Christmas present was weeks in advance, and the time she had cheated on a math test, I was the one she confessed to. I was used to knowing her deepest fears and her greatest joys. What had changed that?

What secret was Mary keeping from me now?

Chapter 13

I dragged myself to school the next day, hardly able to remember that I used to actually like going. Now school was a place where people upset me. I decided to try to concentrate on my classes again. Learning had always given me great joy; maybe that would help me improve my attitude—that, and ignoring all the things that were being said about Mark.

I went to my homeroom as soon as I got to school, not wanting to be in the hallways any longer than necessary. I was sitting there quietly, trying to read a short story assigned for English, when I felt rather than heard someone approach me from behind. When I turned to look, there was Robert.

"Did you see Mary yesterday?" he asked quietly.

"Yes," I said.

"Has she started to wonder who is responsible for Mark's death?" he asked, his face intense.

"How did you know?" I said, studying him. He didn't know Mary very well.

"I know how it works. Once the initial shock and grief wear off a little, the questions start. That's the way it was with me."

Poor Robert. Not only did he have to cope with

coming back here, but now Mark's death was reminding him of his father's. "Does Mary have any idea who Mark was with that night?" His question made me realize that he must have read the paper—or heard the rumors.

"No," I said. "Mark told his parents that he was going out with her, but they had never made plans. Someone picked him up that night, but it wasn't Mary."

"We have to help her," Robert said. Again I was confused by his intensity. "She shouldn't go through life like I have, never knowing the answers."

"The police are working on it," I said. "In fact, I even had to go answer questions."

Robert shook his head. "See what I mean? If the police knew what they were doing, they'd never think that you were holding back on them. No, Cath, we have to do something ourselves. To the police, it's just one case out of hundreds, but to Mary, it's the only one. What are we going to do?"

More and more kids were filtering into homeroom, and I realized that we didn't have the privacy we needed to have this conversation; besides, the warning bell was due to ring. "Let's talk about this at lunch," I said. Robert nodded and got up to leave. As he walked out, I heard a girl in the back of the room say, "Bulldozer Boy! Run anybody down lately?" Robert kept walking, but I wheeled on the girl. She must have noticed my glare.

"What's the matter? Got a problem?" she asked, laughing in my direction.

"His name is Robert," I said, loudly enough for my voice to carry.

"Robert, Bulldozer Boy, what's the difference? God, some people are so sensitive." She cracked her gum; I heard it across the room as if a small-caliber gun had been shot.

"Yes, you're right, Daisy," I said sweetly, turning to face the front of the room.

"Hey, my name's not Daisy. It's Tammy," she whined.

I nodded my head, not bothering to tell her that Daisy was the name of a cow in a book that my mother used to read me when I was little.

By fourth period, I had absorbed more of the day's rumors. It wasn't that I wanted to hear them, because I didn't. It was just that in every class before the bell rang, and in the groups of kids that clogged the hallway, Mark's name came up with amazing regularity. Today's rumors dealt heavily with the memorial service that was being held tomorrow. Of course, the story was that Mark's body was so mutilated that nobody would be allowed to see it, and that was why the service was being kept private. Still, I heard at least fifteen people say that they were going anyway. I wondered if I should call Mark's parents and warn them.

Robert and I both sat through Spanish class, where we had a major test. I'd completely forgotten about it, which sure wasn't like me. It wasn't too bad until I came to subjunctive verb endings. I did the best I could, not especially caring, waiting impatiently for the bell to ring. When it did, Robert and I headed again for the parking lot. Once again our luck held; no teacher asked us where we were going. As we settled into my VW, this time Robert had a lunch of sorts. It looked like Robert had taken about eight slices of bologna and slapped them between two slices of white bread. Brownish-yellow mustard oozed out of the sides. I peeled my orange, refusing Robert's offer of part of his sandwich.

"Okay," Robert finally said after he had devoured a quarter of his sandwich. "Where do we start?"

"I have a list," I said. I had stuck the list I had made for Mary in my notebook, thinking I might add to it as the day went on. I took it out and gave it to Robert.

He read it silently, then turned to look at me. "Cath, this is not what I had in mind."

"Sorry," I said. "Those are just the rumors I've heard."

"You missed the one about Mark having AIDS and not wanting anyone to know so he threw himself in front of the car."

Now it was my turn to stare. "You're right," I said. "That's one I missed—and I'm glad. I'm not sure I should tell Mary that one."

"Oh, you mean you haven't heard?" Robert asked in mock seriousness. "Mary has AIDS, too, and so does her unborn baby."

Great. She'd love that. The fact that she hadn't been eating and had obviously lost weight would help that rumor to grow. "Do you have a plan?" I asked Robert.

"We need information," he said.

"That's easy enough," I said. "Everybody knows everything. All you have to do is listen."

"No, the ones we have to listen to are the ones who aren't talking," Robert said cryptically.

"That's a little more difficult," I said.

"Think about it," Robert said. "If you were involved in Mark's death, either accidentally or intentionally, and you weren't going to go straight to the police, wouldn't you keep a real low profile for a while?"

"I guess," I said, finding it hard to imagine being

78

responsible for someone's death and keeping it a secret.

"We have to start asking questions," he said. "Someone knows little bits and pieces, and we need to find out those and then fit them together."

"You know, we're just assuming that it was someone at this school. What if it wasn't? What if it was a stranger, or someone Mark knew from somewhere else?"

"You're right, but we have to start somewhere, don't we? We have to try." Robert's voice sounded tense again. The last thing I wanted to do was upset him, too, so I agreed. Besides, how could it hurt to ask a few questions?

"You're right," I said. "Who should we talk to?"

We spent the rest of lunch thinking of possibilities. Since Robert hardly knew anyone, he was going to hover around whatever conversations he could find, watching for reactions. I was going to talk to David, a friend of Mark's with whom I had gone out last year a few times, and Tony. Talking to Tony was Robert's suggestion, and I had agreed, even though I didn't want to.

We strode back into school, two people with a mission, agreeing to meet back at my car after school. I had no trouble finding David, who was standing by the wall outside of the library, a favorite senior gathering place. Several other boys were with him, ogling the girls who walked by.

"David," I said, entering the group to stand by him, feeling very out of place. "I just can't believe what happened to Mark." Why waste time with small talk? After all, class started in a few minutes.

"I know, Cath," David said solemnly.

"Do you have any idea who he was with?" I asked, staring at him.

David looked surprised at my question. I guess it was rather abrupt. I'd have to work on my questioning techniques. "I don't have any idea," David answered. "The guys and I have talked about that, and if he wasn't with us or with Mary, we don't know who it could have been."

"You never heard him talk about meeting someone, maybe someone from another school?" I asked.

"Why are you asking me these questions?" David said, his normal nice-guy patience beginning to fray a little.

"It's Mary," I said quickly. "She really wants to know."

"Sorry, Cath," David said, more pleasantly this time. "I don't know a thing."

I walked away from him without even remembering to say goodbye. If I talked to him any longer, I was going to ask him where he had been at 8:00 on Monday night, and that would not be a good move.

It took me until after school to find Tony. Actually, then it was Tony who found me. I was putting the books I didn't need into my locker when he turned the corner and came to stand beside me.

"How are you doing?" he asked.

"I'm okay," I said, continuing to concentrate on my locker.

"How'd it go at the police station?" Well, it sure hadn't taken long to get this conversation pointed in the right direction.

"Fine," I said. "I told Detective Martin the truth. He mainly wanted to know about Mary."

"Mary?" Tony questioned. "Do the police think Mary had something to do with this?"

"I don't know what they think," I snapped. Then, more cautiously, I asked, "Tony, Mark wasn't with Mary the night he was killed. Who could it have been?"

"What difference does it make?" Tony said quickly.

"It makes a lot of difference," I replied.

"Why? It doesn't bring Mark back." Tony was no longer meeting my eyes.

"It might not bring Mark back, but it would put to rest a lot of questions and suspicions," I said firmly.

"Suspicions?" The voice from behind startled me. There was Cyndee, blonde curls and all. "Who has suspicions?" she asked.

"We were talking about Mark," I said shortly.

"The police talked to Catherine, and I guess it got her thinking," Tony explained.

"The police talked to you? Oh, how awful. Did you have to ride in one of those ugly cars?"

Leave it to Cyndee to worry about image. "No," I said shortly. "The police just wanted to find out about Mark's friends. They're trying to figure out who he was with the night he died."

"Oh, Tony, I just can't bear to think about it. I get so upset." Sure enough, tears welled up in her eyes. I watched carefully. Her mascara didn't run. How did she do that? "Please take me home now. You did promise me a ride, you know, on that big, sexy motorcycle of yours." With that, she stroked Tony's arm. I threw the rest of my books into the locker, not caring whether I had homework or not. The slam of the locker door made Cyndee flinch.

"Goodbye," I said semi-sweetly, heading off

down the hall. I wasn't going to continue this conversation no matter how much Robert wanted information.

"Catherine." I heard my name shouted from behind, but I kept walking. Footsteps behind me picked up their pace. "Catherine, listen to me." Tony caught up and walked beside me. "She needs a friend, that's all."

I looked at Tony as if he had sprouted green hair and a third eye. "A friend? Right."

"Tony!" Cyndee's voice carried down the hallway. We both turned to look. She was standing with her hands on her hips, pouting.

"Your friend needs you," I said. Tony looked from me to Cyndee and back again. "You'd better give her that ride you promised."

"Catherine, you don't understand," Tony said.

"That's where you're wrong," I said quietly. "I do understand."

Chapter 14

Robert and I decided to meet at my apartment in an hour. I stopped at the grocery store to get food for dinner, pumped gas into the trusty red VW, and then headed for home. Within three minutes of walking in the door I was in red sweat pants and an oversized sweat shirt with puffins on it. I called Mary and invited her over, thinking it might make her feel better to know that Robert and I were actually trying to get some information. I was opening a bag of sour cream potato chips when the doorbell donged. It was Robert, and I was glad I could quickly explain my reasons for also inviting Mary. He agreed that it was a good idea.

"Right after my father died, I felt isolated from the rest of the world. I think people were afraid they didn't know the right thing to say or that they might upset me, so they ended up avoiding me. It was terrible. It was part of the reason why I stopped talking."

I smiled, then regretted it when I saw confusion wrinkle Robert's brow. "I'm not smiling at you," I explained. "It's just that Mary loves to talk. I don't think there's much danger of her stopping for long."

"Good for her," Robert said.

With that, the doorbell donged again and the object of our discussion appeared. She definitely seemed to be making some progress. Although she was still pale, her cheeks now had a little color again, and her eyes were clear and alert. She didn't look happy, but she did look more focused and energetic than she had. Another good sign was that she immediately reached for a handful of potato chips. Mary loves food, and the fact that she hadn't been eating had been one of my many concerns about her lately.

"Do you have any soda?" she asked.

I was happy to get it for her, as well as glasses for Robert and myself. When I got back to the living room from the kitchen, Mary and Robert were sitting on the sofa, talking quietly. I could hear Robert filling Mary in on his father's death.

"How terrible that must have been," Mary said in a very subdued tone of voice. "I know how terrible it has been losing Mark, but that's still not as bad as losing your only parent."

"We both feel great pain," Robert said. "Who's to measure which pain is greater?"

Mary nodded in agreement. For a moment, I felt like an outsider. Robert seemed to be finding the words to help Mary better than I had been able to. Who ever would have thought? I observed them carefully as I curled up in the chair, knees pulled up so my chin could rest on them. They were such a study in opposites—Mary usually bubbling over with laughter and lunacy, Robert mulling over life in silence.

"Cath, tell me about school today." It was almost a shock when Mary interrupted my observation to include me in the conversation.

"Should I tell her the medical news?" I asked Robert.

"I guess she'll find out eventually," he said with a smile.

"Mary, I don't quite know how to break this to you, but Mark, you, and your unborn baby all have AIDS."

I hadn't been sure how Mary would react, and I was relieved when after a few seconds of stunned silence she began to laugh. Robert and I joined in.

Robert then explained to her our theory about trying to get information around school, and Mary seemed immediately pleased.

"Actually, you should be able to provide the most information," Robert said to her.

"Just what is that supposed to mean?" snapped Mary, her good mood instantaneously disappearing.

"You certainly knew Mark better than either of us," Robert replied calmly.

"But I wasn't with him on Monday night," Mary said, her voice still sharp.

"I didn't say you were," Robert said, his voice still soft.

"Then how would I know anything?"

"You know Mark's habits—where he was likely to go, who he was likely to see. Mary, that's all I meant."

"Well I don't know where he was that night." I watched Mary with growing concern. Her hands were shaking slightly, and she clenched them.

"Was there anywhere Mark typically went on Monday nights—a meeting, the library, the mall?" Robert pursued his questions.

"A meeting? What do you think he was, some kind of Boy Scout?" The sarcasm in Mary's voice had a nasty edge. I didn't like the way this was going.

"Mary, Robert is just trying to figure out where we should go next to get information. He's trying to help."

"Well, I've had enough."

"I'm sorry," Robert said. "I didn't mean to upset you."

"I'm not upset," Mary snapped.

Right, I thought. "I've got an idea," I said brightly. "Why don't we fix dinner together?"

"I'm not hungry," Mary said. "I'm going home. I'm going to Mark's memorial service tomorrow."

"Maybe you'll be able to talk to his parents," Robert said.

"You never give up, do you?" she said, glaring at him.

"Not until I have to," Robert replied, never losing his quiet focus.

I walked Mary to the door. "Do you want me to go with you tomorrow?" I asked.

"No," she said. "I have to do this alone."

It seemed like she was feeling that way more and more these days. I tried to give her a hug, but she quickly pulled away from me and walked down the steps. She was halfway down the flight when she turned and called back up to me. "You know, Cath, it's weird that bad things started happening right after Robert came back to town." Before I could respond, she was gone. I heard the door on the first floor shut behind her. I started after her in amazement, hoping that her voice had not carried back to Robert. I didn't think it had.

"I'm sorry," I said to Robert as I flopped back down in the chair.

"Don't apologize," he said. "She's just upset."

The next words hurt to say; I felt like I was betraying all my years of friendship with Mary. "Are you sure that's all she is?"

Robert rubbed his temples before he spoke. "You mean you don't know where Mary was on Monday night?"

"She won't tell me," I said, feeling both fear and sadness well up inside of me.

"Cath, I really don't think Mary had anything to do with Mark's death." Was that the truth, or was Robert trying to humor me?

"Neither do I," I said, wishing that a trace of doubt wasn't nagging at me. What kind of friend was I?

The phone rang, and I almost welcomed the interruption, at least until I found out who it was. My father's call from California was not likely to cheer me up.

"How are you?" he asked.

"I'm okay, Dad," I replied. "I'm spending time with Mary, and I'm going to school, and the apartment is fine."

"Have you heard from your mother?"

"Yes, and she and Mr. Donelly are having a great time. How's the office coming?"

"You wouldn't believe how complicated it has all become." My father rambled on for several minutes about computer hookups and weight-bearing beams and productivity schedules.

"Well, you'd better get back to work," I said when there was an interruption. I didn't want him to start asking about who had answered the phone before, even though that seemed like ancient history after all that had happened since.

"Are you sure you don't want me to come home?" my father asked.

"No, Dad, there's nothing you could do here. Finish your job." I knew that was what he wanted to hear; it also happened to be the truth.

We said our goodbyes, and I sighed with relief. The longer I didn't have to explain why Robert had answered the phone, the better the chances that my father would forget.

I needed to be active, to chase away the questions for a while. "I hope you don't think I'm fixing dinner by myself," I called in to Robert. "If you want to eat, you'd better get yourself out to this kitchen."

He quickly joined me. I scrubbed two baking potatoes, pierced them, and put them on a paper towel in the microwave. I handed Robert a plastic bag full of green beans. "How about snapping these?" I asked.

"Sure," he said, then stood there holding the bag, staring at it stupidly.

"First you need to rinse them off in the sink," I said. "Then you can snap them into this." I got a cooking pot.

Obediently he dumped the beans into the sink and turned on the water full force. After a minute or two, I turned the water off. I watched him stare at the beans before I finally took mercy on him. "Never snapped beans before?" I asked.

"The only beans I know come out of a box in the freezer," he admitted.

I showed him how to break off both ends, discard those, and then break the beans into uniform sized-pieces. He was slow, but eventually the beans were in the pot and cooking. Next I gave him the lettuce, tomato, green pepper, and mushrooms for a salad while I pounded out two chicken breasts to sauté with butter and lemon. I had to tell him to tear the lettuce rather than cut it, to core the tomato, and to scrub the mushrooms. He did pretty well with the green pepper. Luckily he took my teasing well. By some miracle, all of the parts of the dinner got finished within five minutes of each other, and we were eating at the dining room table when the doorbell rang.

Tony was standing there when I opened the door. From where he was, he could see into the dining room.

"I was worried that you were upset when you left school today, but obviously you're fine. How cozy. Does he live here?" Tony's voice was quiet but sarcastic.

"I wasn't upset," I said, stepping out into the hallway and pulling the door shut behind me.

"Well, if you were, you've certainly made a fine recovery. Don't let me interrupt." With that, Tony turned around and headed down the steps. I started to call after him that Robert had his own apartment now, but I stopped myself. I didn't owe Tony any explanations.

I heard the first floor door slam, and I had to smile. If I hadn't known better, I would have sworn that Tony was jealous.

I went back to Robert and finished a dinner that tasted even better than it had before.

Robert was good company. We even laughed over doing the dishes. When he finally said that he needed to be going, I was sorry to see him go. He was easy to be around, and I loved to make him laugh. He had a great laugh, low and husky. The fact that he didn't laugh much made it sound even better when he did.

Chapter 15

The fact that it was Friday made it easier to get out of bed and face the day. I had put on jeans, a turtleneck, and a heavy ski sweater, but I still shivered as I scraped the frost off of the VW's windows and waited for it to warm up. I wondered what the weather was like in Ireland. I was glad that my mother was having such a good time. Eight more days and she would be home. Maybe by then life would be back to normal. That was a comforting thought.

At school I kept listening, although by now people were talking about subjects other than Mark's death. Still, the memorial service was today, and that kept the topic on some people's minds. I also asked questions when I could. That seemed to surprise some of the kids. I guess they were used to my being the quiet one who was always on the outer edge of their conversations. They had paid plenty of amazed attention when I was dating Tony, and they were used to seeing me with Mary, who knew them all, but by myself I still was not a focus of much interest. That was fine with me.

As I sat in second period waiting for my English class to start, I heard two guys behind me mention

Mark. I turned slightly, thinking I heard one say something about Mark knowing how to have a good time. With that, David walked in, and came up to chat with the guys.

They said something I couldn't hear to him, and David replied, "Yeah, I wish I knew his secret."

I turned around the rest of the way, and smiled at David. "What secret is that?" I asked sweetly, trying to keep smiling and make it sound like an innocent question.

"Nothing," David said quickly. "Hi, Cath. I didn't realize you were sitting there."

"What secret?" I asked again. The other two guys were now staring at me, and my face flushed with embarrassment.

David stammered as he replied. "What made Mark so popular," he finally said.

"Yeah, popular is one word for it," said one of the guys.

"Lucky is a better word," said the other. They snickered at each other. The teacher began to call roll, and David escaped to his seat.

I tried to concentrate on the Chekhov story we were discussing, but it wasn't easy. I couldn't wait until fourth period when I could talk to Robert. Maybe the guys hadn't meant anything, but somehow I doubted that. If they considered Mark lucky, that must have something to do with girls. David was a nice guy, but I vaguely knew the reputations of the other two. They were the kind who claimed to have slept with the entire cheer-leading squad.

Robert was late getting to Spanish class, so I didn't have a chance to talk to him until after class when we could go have our now-customary lunch in my car.

"Let me dump some of these books in my locker," I said as we walked out of class. "My morning teachers were kind-hearted enough not to give homework over the weekend." Robert followed as I turned down the hallway that led to my locker. When I was within a few steps, I saw the corner of a note sticking out of the door of it. For a second I smiled, thinking it was a note from Mary, a familiar occurrence since Mary always had exciting news she couldn't wait to tell me. Then the smile quickly faded. Mary wasn't in school today. The only other person who had ever left notes stuck in my locker was Tony, and that was back when we were dating. Maybe that was it. Maybe he was sorry about storming away last night and saying those things about Robert. Again the smile was on my lips. How nice—and how unusual—of Tony to admit that he had been wrong. Meanwhile, I was standing in front of my locker staring at the note.

"Cath, let's get going. We only have a half hour." Robert's voice jolted me out of my reverie. I pulled the note out, then unlocked my locker and dumped my books into the top section. I unfolded the note as Robert and I began to walk toward the back exit of the school. What I saw made me stop as if an invisible wall had appeared in front of us. Robert didn't notice that I had stopped until he was ten or twelve steps beyond me. Then he looked for me, spinning around when I wasn't beside him.

As he started back to where I was rooted in the hallway, I lurched into motion again.

"What is it, Cath?" he called.

I didn't answer but rather began to run for the doorway. I didn't stop running until I was in the parking lot and at my car. Then my hands were shaking so badly that I couldn't get the key in the lock. Robert caught up to me and took the keys from my hand. He unlocked the door, and I gratefully crawled into the worn bucket seat. He went to the other side, unlocked his door, and was soon beside me. Wordlessly he took the note that I was still clutching. It was a sheet of unlined paper, and on it was printed in black capital letters:

IF YOU KNOW WHAT'S GOOD FOR YOU, YOU'LL STOP ASKING SO MANY QUESTIONS.

"This is great," Robert said happily.

"Great? I get a death threat and you think it's great?" How could he say such a thing?

"No, Cath, think about it."

"I don't want to think about it."

Robert spoke in his infuriatingly calm way. "This means we're on the right track. This means that someone here at school knows something. We've touched a nerve."

"And whoever knows something also knows who I am and where my locker is." I was not finding this quite as wonderful as Robert was.

"Cath, it's just a warning."

"Great. And what am I supposed to do about it?"

"Keep asking questions."

"Robert, I'm not some kind of Nancy Drew detective. This scares me. I don't want to deal with it."

Robert studied me carefully before he spoke. "Are you ready to give up?"

"No," I answered. "I just think that maybe I better tell Detective Martin about this. He's the professional."

"Do you really think he'd take you seriously?" Robert's question made me think about going to the police to explain this whole situation. Somehow the note didn't seem quite as dramatic as it had before.

"Okay, what's your suggestion?" I asked.

"Maybe you'd better stay out of this, and I'll keep working on it."

"No way." The thought of being excluded bothered me more than the threat.

"Cath, I don't want to see you in any danger."

"I think it's already too late for that," I said. "Besides, I'm sure you're right. It's just a warning. It's not like the note threatens to blow up my car or mutilate my dog or something."

"Cath, you don't have a dog."

"Will you stop being so logical? It's just an example." I glared at him, but my glare quickly relaxed into a smile.

"There's something else good about that note that we've missed," Robert said.

"I've never known anyone to find so much good in one nasty sentence," I said. "What is it this time?"

"Mary's not in school today, so that leaves her out of this."

I sure hadn't thought of that angle. Robert was right. Anything that would rid me of my doubts about my best friend was definitely good. Thinking of Mary made me remember the conversation in second period, and I quickly filled Robert in on the talk with David and the other two guys.

"Do you think one of them could have left the note?" Robert asked.

"I don't know," I answered. "I wonder when it was put in my locker?"

"You didn't use it earlier?"

"Not since before homeroom."

"It could have been after second period, then."

My mind was swirling with possibilities, but there didn't seem to be any solid facts to anchor them.

Robert and I were so caught up in throwing out ideas to each other that we forgot to eat our lunches. The sound of the warning bell jolted us back to the practicalities of school, and we dashed back to the building, agreeing to meet at the end of the day.

"Be careful, Cath," Robert warned as I headed for the doorway of my fifth period class. I smiled back at him.

"Look around. There are fourteen hundred people in this building. I don't exactly think anything is going to happen to me here." I went into class with seconds to spare. How strange, I thought as I sat down. Now I'm the one reassuring Robert.

I tried to find David between classes but had no success. I wondered if he was avoiding me, but then I decided that was giving myself too much credit. It was a big building. He could be any number of places for any number of reasons.

I was on my way to seventh period when I got my biggest shock of the day, a shock that upset me even more than the note. I was stuck behind a group of about six girls who were walking slowly down the hallway, effectively blocking me from getting around them. They weren't aware that I was close behind them, waiting for a chance to get by. The only one I recognized was Cyndee, whose presence made me glance around for Tony. I was getting used to seeing her draped over him.

"Have you heard the latest?" I heard her say. "I heard that Cath Berry is being questioned by the police about Mark's murder."

I almost spoke up right then. She was right; I had been questioned, but it wasn't any big deal. I could set her straight right now.

"They think she was with Mark the night he died."

Now where had Cyndee gotten that idea? How ridiculous. What would I have been doing with Mark?

"Cath Berry?" one of the other girls asked. "What would Mark have been doing with *her*?"

I didn't know whether to be pleased or insulted.

"I thought she was Mary's best friend," another girl added.

"That little bitch," said a third with what almost seemed to be admiration.

I was so amazed that I couldn't figure out what to do. Finally I did nothing. I walked into my seventh period class and sat there in a daze. I'd always known that rumors had lives of their own, totally separate from reality. Still, I'd never been quite so personally involved, and I didn't like it one little bit.

Robert was right. We needed to keep working on this.

Chapter 16

I was still in a daze by the end of the period, and I didn't say a word to anybody until I met Robert beside my car.

"Robert, I overhead some girls talking about me."

"You certainly have become a hot topic," he said quietly.

"What's that supposed to mean?" I asked sharply.

"I heard someone say that you'd gotten a death threat."

"You're kidding! Who knew about that note besides you and me? Did you say anything?"

"No," Robert answered. "Who would I tell?"

"Well, I certainly didn't say a word about it," I said, lapsing into puzzled silence.

"What did you hear?" Robert finally asked.

I told him about Cyndee's conversation.

"This is amazing. In one day, you've become a sleaze and the object of a death threat. Way to go, Cath."

I knew he was trying to make me feel better, but he wasn't helping.

"Robert, this doesn't make sense. If I was

somehow involved in Mark's death, why would I warn myself not to ask so many questions?"

"That's your problem, Cath. You want things to make sense. My guess would be that the two rumors are coming from different sources that haven't met up yet."

"Thank heavens it's the weekend," I said. "Maybe some of this will die down by Monday."

"You really are a dreamer, aren't you?" Robert said with a smile. Then he turned more serious. "You know, Cath, I feel bad about this. I was the one who wanted you to ask questions, and now look what has happened. I feel responsible. I'd much rather that I were the target of this rather than you."

"You can't change what has happened. Besides, you didn't force me into this. I could have said no. I have to accept responsibility for my own actions."

"I'd feel a little better if I followed you home and made sure there were no more weird notes," Robert said.

"It's a deal. I'll wait for you to get your car." If the truth be told, I was glad that he was going home with me. I could talk a good game about accepting responsibility, but that didn't mean I wanted to walk into an empty apartment. Part of me wished that my mother was home. It would be comforting to have her around. Another part of me was glad that she was away. She would have a fit if she knew I was in any remote way in danger, and she would put a stop to what I was doing. Yes, Mom was better off in Ireland. By the time she got home, this would have all blown over—I hoped.

Robert's car soon appeared in my rearview mirror, and he followed me home. We walked up to the apartment building together, stopping in the first floor entranceway to get the mail. I unlocked the mailbox and pulled out a stack of bills and grocery store flyers. Nothing was stuck in there that was the least bit unusual. Then we went up to the second floor and my door. Again, nothing seemed out of the ordinary. I unlocked the door and looked around, Robert right behind me. I have to admit that my heart was beating just a little bit faster then it should have been.

"Robert, I feel like an absolute fool, but will you do me a favor?"

"What?" Robert asked cautiously.

"Will you look under the beds and behind the shower curtain?"

"This is getting to you, isn't it?" Robert was studying me in a way that made me even more nervous.

"I think I've watched too many movies," I admitted sheepishly. "Never mind. It was a stupid request."

"No, I'll do it," Robert said, but he didn't move.

"Want me to go with you?" I asked.

"No, that's okay. I'll do it myself." Still he didn't move.

"Wait. Let me find you a weapon." I had begun to whisper, suddenly realizing that if there was someone hiding in the apartment, it would be better to keep our plan a secret.

"Cath, I don't think that's necessary." Still, Robert didn't move, and I noticed that he was whispering, too.

"No, I insist. Since I'm making you do this, the least I can do is arm you." I tiptoed to the closet by the door and slowly, quietly pushed open its door. I searched through the bottom of it looking for a baseball bat. That would be the perfect weapon. The only problem was that neither my mother nor

Mr. Donelly nor I had ever, to my knowledge, played baseball. Why would there be a bat? All I could find was a Frisbee and a tennis racquet. I held out the tennis racquet to Robert with an inquiring look. He shook his head, so I put it back in the closet.

"I've got it," I whispered, motioning for him to follow me. This time I headed for the kitchen. I opened the drawer that held our miscellaneous kitchen utensils. First I pulled out a small wooden mallet we used to crack open crabs. Robert laughed out loud, and I hushed him. A quick look in the pantry yielded a large can of creamed corn. That was it. I handed it to Robert, who looked at me in amazement.

"I can see the headlines now," he whispered. "'Girl's Attacker Creamed by Corn-Wielding Colleague.'"

This time I was the one who laughed. Feeling more than a little silly, I followed Robert, at the last second grabbing a can of chicken noodle soup myself. The first door we got to on the left was the bathroom. Robert walked in, looked behind the door, and then dramatically flung back the shower curtain. Nothing was there but some blue tile that, to my embarrassment had a definite buildup of soap scum. I backed up so that Robert could lead the way out. The next door on the left was mine. I almost told Robert to forget that one, afraid that I had left stray underwear strewn around. Still, safety would have to come first. He stalked into the room, can of corn hefted aloft in his right hand. A quick look around revealed nothing but my normal clutter. Robert kneeled beside my bed and peered underneath. With his left hand he reached under and swept out my stuffed dog Jingles that I had owned since I was a child, a copy of *Cosmopolitan* that I had borrowed from my mother's room, and three shoes. Nothing too dangerous there. I was even confident enough to open my closet door myself. Anyone would have to be a midget to hide in there among all the shoes and boxes and books and clothes.

That left my mother's room. I had to mentally remind myself that it was also Mr. Donelly's room. I didn't feel quite right prowling around in there with Robert, but it was for a good cause. Another under-bed search and closet sweep revealed nothing but a few signs that I had inherited my lack of neatness from my mother.

"Thanks," I whispered to Robert. "I feel much better now."

"Why are you whispering?" he whispered back.

"You're right," I said in a normal tone of voice. I looked sheepishly at the can of soup in my hand. Robert handed me the corn, and we both walked back to the kitchen.

"I could stay here if you'd feel better," Robert said as I returned the cans to the pantry.

"What's there to be afraid of?" I asked. "I feel perfectly safe now that I know there's nobody hiding in here. I don't need a babysitter." Even as I spoke, I went to the sliding glass door in the living room and tested to make sure that it was locked. I pulled the curtains, even though it was still early in the afternoon.

"Really, Cath, just let me call my aunt. I was supposed to go have dinner there tonight, but I think I'd feel better if I stayed here with you."

"And I would feel like a fool. Nothing is going to happen. It was just a silly note, probably somebody's idea of a sick joke. Go. Tell your aunt I said hello.''

"Let me leave her number for you. If you hear anything, if anything at all happens, call me there and I'll come right over. Do you want me to come check on you on my way home?''

"No. Thanks, but I think I'll go to bed early. Don't worry about me. This is all silly. Can you imagine what would have happened if there really had been someone in here? He would have laughed himself to death at the sight of us armed with canned goods.''

Robert laughed with me, but he still wrote down the phone number on the pad on the kitchen counter. I shoved him out the door before he could fuss any more.

Once he was gone, I realized how quiet the apartment was. Every footstep in the hallway suddenly seemed to echo hollowly. Still, that was easy to solve. I turned on the television, using the remote control to scan through the stations. Finally I settled on MTV with the volume up. Thirty seconds later I realized that I was too keyed up to sit still. Turning the volume up even louder I went to my room. At least I might as well do something productive. I started picking up clothes, magazines, books and other assorted belongings. I even dusted, vacuumed, and cleaned out the bottom of my closet. I started to sort out my underwear drawer but decided that was overkill. An hour later, my room looked better than it had in years. I wanted to seal it up until my mother got home so that I could enjoy her amazement.

The effort had taken the edge off my energy, and it felt good to flop down on the sofa. This time I changed the channel to the news, then went to the door to retrieve the newspaper. For some reason I like to read the newspaper while I watch the news. A McDonalds commercial reminded me that I hadn't eaten, so I went to look around in the refrigerator. Nothing looked too appealing except some ice cream. I put the jar of chocolate sauce in the microwave to heat while I scooped out a big bowl of French vanilla ice cream. Calcium is important, I rationalized, as I spooned on the hot sauce. What a great dinner—and only one dish to wash.

By the time *Jeopardy* came on at 7:00, I was content and relaxed. I enjoyed round one of the game even though I only knew about five answers, and they were lucky guesses. The commercials that preceded round two had just ended when the doorbell rang. I jumped up to answer the door, still glancing back to the television.

"How could you just open the door like that?" Tony's angry face and voice greeted me.

"It was easy," I shot back. "I just turned the knob and pulled."

"Catherine, you know what I mean." He stepped inside the door and I shut it behind him, not wanting to entertain the neighbors with this conversation.

"No, I don't Tony. Why don't you explain it to me?"

"I heard about the threats."

I honestly had put that out of my mind. "What threats, Tony?" I might as well find out what the rumors had grown to by now.

"Don't play cute with me. I heard that a note was left in your locker threatening to kill you if you didn't stop asking questions." Tony was yelling at me as if I'd done something wrong.

"Well, you're half right, no, actually two thirds. That's not bad." I was really not pleased with his attitude. "There was a note in my locker, and it did warn me to stop asking questions. It was not a death threat, though. Just a warning."

"Just a warning? Just a warning?" Tony's voice had jumped an octave. "Let me see the note."

"Tony, will you calm down? It's no big deal."

"Let me decide about that. Where's the note, Catherine?"

Maybe it would calm him down if he saw it. I walked to the coffee table where my books had ended up. There it was, stuck in the front of my Spanish book. I handed it to Tony with a sigh, then sat down on the sofa.

"I don't like this, Catherine," he said, pacing back and forth in front of me. "Why are you asking questions, anyway?"

"I want to know who killed Mark," I said simply.

"Why can't you accept that it was an accident of some kind?" Tony asked, still angry.

"I just want to know who he was with. More importantly, I want Mary to know what happened. I think it will make it easier for her to let go of her grief if she has some answers."

"Well it's not going to help Mary if something happens to you. That's all she needs."

"Tony, nothing is going to happen. Look at me. I'm fine."

"For now," Tony said, stopping in front of me.

There was something in his tone of voice that I didn't like. "What is that supposed to mean?" I asked. "Do you know something that I don't?"

"No," Tony answered, but he answered too quickly.

"Come on, Tony, if you know something about this note, or about Mark's death, I want to know. I deserve to know." I got to my feet and grabbed his arm to stop his pacing. "Level with me, Tony. What do you know?"

"Nothing, Catherine. I told you that. It's just that if you keep asking questions and if there is someone around who's hiding something about Mark's death, you're going to make that person pretty unhappy."

"Unhappy enough to kill me, too? Is that what you mean, Tony?" I grabbed Tony's other arm, anchoring him, making him face me.

"I don't know, Catherine. I just don't want anything to happen to you."

"I don't want anything to happen to me, either," I said firmly.

"Then let it rest," Tony said.

"No," I answered.

"You are a stubborn, hard-headed fool." Tony reach out to grab my arms and give me a gentle shake.

"You always did know just what to say to a girl." I pulled my arms free.

"Come here," Tony said, putting his arms around me and pulling me tight against his chest. I kept my arms doubled up in front of me, distancing him, then relented and reached up to put my arms around his neck. He hugged me fiercely, almost to the point where I feared for my ribs.

"I can see the headlines now," I said in a muffled voice. "'Girl Hugged to Death.'"

"There are worse ways to go," Tony said, but he also let go of me.

"I appreciate your concern," I said.

"I had to be sure you were all right," Tony said. He glanced at his watch. "I have to go. Are you sure you're okay?"

Where did he have to go? "I'm sure," I said.

"Will you lock the door behind me?" he asked.

"I'll lock the door behind you."

"And not just throw open the door for anybody who rings the bell?"

"I'll be careful," I said, wondering if he would stay if I told him that I was scared.

"Goodbye, Catherine. Don't forget to lock the door."

"I won't."

He opened the door, then shut it behind him. I didn't hear his footsteps leave until after I had turned the deadbolt.

Where did he have to go?

Chapter 17

My sleep was filled with bad dreams that night, dreams that featured Tony, Mary, and a supporting cast of hundreds chasing me down a dark street while Robert tried to trip them by rolling cans of creamed corn at their feet. I was glad to finally awake with sunlight streaming through my bedroom window.

Saturday stretched in front of me with no plans. There were plenty of things I could do—homework, housework, grocery shopping—but they weren't things that I wanted to do. I needed to check on Mary since I hadn't talked to her yesterday. Granted she was being difficult, but I wasn't about to give up on her. Our friendship had lasted too long to stop counting on it now. I wanted to talk to Robert, too, to see what theories he had about a next step. It didn't seem like we should go for two whole days without trying to do something to get more information. It was still too early to call either one, though, so I made myself a mug of hot chocolate and went back to bed with a copy of a Stephen King book that I had promised myself I would only read in broad daylight.

Ten pages later, the phone rang. I reluctantly

closed the book and went to the kitchen. Mary's voice greeted my hello.

"Cath, can we go for a walk?"

"Sure. Want me to come to your house?"

"No, I'll come to you. Fifteen minutes?" She didn't even wait for an answer before she hung up.

I went back to my room, and with a last longing glance at Stephen King, grabbed a pair of black sweat pants, and my heavy grey University of Delaware sweat shirt. I was stepping into my Reeboks when the doorbell rang. I grabbed a jacket and my keys and was ready to go.

Mary's hair was pulled back into a short ponytail, making her cheekbones look even more pronounced. She has beautiful features, and with her lean, tall body, I've often thought she should be a model. I always feel like a dwarf in comparison. I took a quick look at her eyes, trying to read her mood. I found no clues since she refused to look at me. Still, I was hopeful. For years now, whenever one of us has something that really needs to be talked out, we ask the other one to go for a walk. It has become a signal that one of us is in bad need of a friend to talk to. There have been times when we've walked miles and miles, hardly knowing where we were by the time we hashed out the problem, only to find that the problem was resolved but that we now had miles and miles to walk to get home again.

We struck off at a brisk pace, the silence lengthening. Mary had requested the walk; eventually she would have to explain the reason. She knew the rules.

"Cath, the memorial service was nice. A minister spoke, and then Mark's uncle. But somehow it didn't seem like it was really Mark they were talking about. I kept expecting him to walk in and sit beside me and take my hand and whisper something funny in my ear. It just doesn't seem like it can really be over.''

I didn't know what to say, so I just kept walking.

"I mean, my mind knows that Mark is . . . dead, but I still keep thinking I hear him, that the phone will ring and it will be him."

"I'm so sorry, Mary."

"I know, and I know that I haven't been fair to you. That's why I wanted to talk to you now."

"Don't worry about me," I said. "I know how much you've been through. I understand."

"That's why I feel even worse about the way I've treated you. You're my best friend in the world. I need you. I can't stand to think that you don't believe in me."

"Mary, I believe in you."

"I wouldn't blame you if you didn't. I think I've just been in such pain myself, that I wanted to make other people suffer, too. I know that's stupid, but I haven't been able to make sense of much of anything."

"It's okay," I said, trying to soothe her.

"No it's not, Cath. I want to explain."

"You don't have to."

"That's exactly why I do have to, Cath. I want to tell you where I was the night Mark was killed. I just need for you to promise me first that you won't hate me."

"Mary, I promise I won't hate you."

"I had an appointment Monday night. I wanted to tell you, in fact I wanted you to go with me, but I was afraid that you would think I was a terrible person." She stopped then, and I wanted to shake her to get her started again. We walked ten steps, fifteen steps, twenty steps.

"Mary, the only way I will hate you is if you don't tell me the rest now that you've started."

"I had an appointment at the Planned Parenthood Center." Mary said the words in a rush, and then started walking even faster so that I had to break into a jog to keep up with her long legs.

"Is that all?" I said. "What a relief."

"What do you mean, is that all? After the promise I made to you last year, I thought you would hate me."

"What promise, Mary?" She made a lot of promises to me, most of which she broke.

"That I wouldn't ever have sex again as long as I lived."

Now I remembered. Mary had been convinced last year that she was pregnant. We had both nearly lost our sanity before she found out that it was a false scare. That was right—she had promised me that she would never again create that possibility.

"Say something, Cath."

"I remember," I said. "What changed your mind?" Suddenly I stopped and grabbed her so that she had to stop, too. "You're not . . ."

"No, I'm not pregnant," she said before I could finish. "It's just that I found myself thinking more and more about making love with Mark, and I couldn't face another one of those scares, so I wanted to go get information about birth control. We didn't do anything, Cath. We were just thinking about it."

"Mary, I understand. You're certainly not a bad person for thinking about it, and you're not a bad person for wanting to be responsible."

"Would you have gone with me to Planned Parenthood if I had asked?"

"Of course I would have."

"It sure would have saved us both a lot of grief," she said with a shake of her head.

Suddenly more questions were bombarding my brain. "Mary, did you tell Detective Martin the truth?"

"Yes," Mary answered, and I sighed with relief. "Do you think I'm totally crazy? He's a detective. I knew better than to lie to him. Besides, he promised that he wouldn't tell my parents."

"Why did you want to claim that you were with me that night?"

"When I left to go to my appointment that night, I told my parents I was going out with you. I couldn't exactly tell them the truth. I mean, they still think I'm their little girl. I didn't think it would go over too well if I announced that I was going to get information on birth control. Besides, if my father knew what I was thinking about, he'd send me to a nunnery or lock me in my room for the next few years."

This was the Mary I knew and loved. "Mary, I don't think you're giving your parents quite enough credit."

"It was hard enough telling Detective Martin the truth, and I'm not exactly enjoying telling you. Give me a break, Cath."

"I'm sorry. So Detective Martin believed you."

"He didn't have to. He called Planned Parenthood, and they verified that I had been there, which meant that I couldn't have been with Mark."

I was flooded with guilt. How could I ever have doubted Mary? "I'm so sorry," I said, tears filling my eyes.

"About what?" Mary asked, confused.

"About ever doubting you," I admitted.

"Did you really think I could have had something

to do with Mark's death?'' I knew Mary had to ask that, and I knew that I had to answer it honestly.

"I knew that you would never harm him deliberately. I guess I was just afraid that you two were having another one of your arguments and some bizarre accident happened." There. The words were said. I felt like our friendship was hanging in the balance. I wouldn't blame Mary for hating me.

"I don't blame you," Mary said quietly. "I don't like the fact that you doubted me, but I gave you plenty of reasons, especially when I asked you to lie for me. I wasn't thinking clearly, and I felt like if my parents were upset with me on top of everything else, I just couldn't stand it."

"I wish you'd told me the truth earlier, but I understand."

"I always believed you would." Mary and I had stopped walking, and we hugged each other, not noticing the wondering looks of the people in passing cars. I felt a hundred pounds lighter.

"Come on, I thought we were going for a walk." Mary's words got us moving again, and we set off at a brisk pace. The cool October air felt good against my cheeks, and the leaves crunched underfoot.

Maybe everything wasn't solved, but this sure helped.

Chapter 18

By the time Mary and I walked back to my apartment again, my feet were sore but my heart was happy. For the very first time since all of this had begun, I felt like Mary and I were all right with each other. She had told me about Monday night, and I had told her about the note in my locker and Robert and Tony. There were no more secrets, no more tensions. We even decided to go to the mall. Mary called it a practice for school on Monday. Sure enough, a group of kids we vaguely recognized from school stopped dead in their tracks, stared at Mary, and then began to whisper frantically. Then I realized I might be making the wrong assumption. After yesterday's rumors, the whispering might be about me.

I could see Mary's mouth tighten, and her eyes became hard and cold. Still, though, she kept her composure. No one actually approached her to talk, although that would undoubtedly change in school. We forced ourselves to walk the entire length of the mall and then back again. We even forced ourselves to do it without buying anything. It was a test of character for both of us, and we did survive it. By the time we got back to my apartment, Mary had to leave, having promised her parents she'd be home by early afternoon. I curled up on the sofa with my book, only to find myself waking up three hours later, the book still on my stomach. Either the walk or the relief had knocked me out. Now I was hungry.

I fixed myself a huge baked potato with lots of sour cream and then had a bowl of ice cream. It was a good thing my mother wasn't around to yell at me about the menus I was creating.

This time I stayed awake reading; in fact, I stayed too awake. Suddenly I was hearing noises in the quiet apartment, seeing shadows in the darkness outside the windows. I threw down the book. This would not do. I needed to get out.

I knew that Robert didn't have a phone yet, so I decided to walk down to his apartment. I threw a jacket over my sweater and locked the door behind me. I was almost to Robert's building when I saw him walking toward his car.

"Robert," I called.

He spun around quickly. "Cath, what are you doing here?"

"I just needed some company," I said, "but if you're on your way out, I don't want to keep you."

"That's okay," he said. He seemed nervous, though, not at all like his normal, contained self. "I can change my plans."

"Robert, what are you up to?" I asked. I was in the mood for honesty even if my question was rather rude.

"I don't want you involved in this," he said, looking down at the ground. "I don't want there to be any more danger for you."

"Come on, Robert. Level with me." He was making me both curious and worried.

"Do you promise you'll stay out it?"

"No," I answered promptly.

"I'll see you later, then," he said, reaching for his car's door handle.

"No way," I said, blocking his arm.

"Cath, I'm going to the parking lot of Duffy's Tavern," Robert said, giving in. "I just want to see where it happened."

"That's a good idea," I said. "Unlock the door on my side."

"I'll tell you what. I'll stop at your place on my way back and tell you about it."

By this time, I had discovered that the passenger-side door was unlocked anyway, and I sat in the car waiting for Robert.

"I don't like this," he said.

"You'll get over it," I answered. "Drive."

He was silent as he drove, but I didn't figure I'd better push him any further. I hadn't been near Main Street since before Mark's death, and I started to get more and more uneasy the closer we got to Duffy's Tavern.

It was Robert who broke the silence. "I just want to see. I'm not saying we'll find out anything."

"That's okay," I said. I didn't even want to see the place, but since I'd made him bring me, I couldn't very well complain now. The entrance to the parking lot split off Main Street to the left. Robert turned in, passed the side of the tavern, and drove into the parking lot itself. A shiver passed through me. Robert found a parking space and pulled in, then cut the engine.

For the first few minutes, I didn't want to look, didn't want to visualize Mark's body. After I had memorized every detail on the dashboard, though, I finally looked up. Nothing seemed unusual about the parking lot. There were maybe fifty slots lined off, and on either side were fences separating this lot from those behind the stores on either side. Robert got out out of the car and leaned against the side. I got out and walked over to lean beside him.

"Wait here," Robert said, walking away.

I followed a few steps behind him as he walked up to a doorway at the back of the tavern. A wooden door was propped open, and Robert pulled open the screen door and stuck his head inside.

"Excuse me," he said politely. "Were you working here Monday night?"

I looked over Robert's shoulder at a frazzled man maybe 25 years old. His curly hair tumbled to his shoulders, and his arms were leanly muscled below his rolled-up T-shirt sleeves. He was scraping a large metal spatula over the surface of a large grill. He turned to face us, his face surly.

"Look, I'm sick of all these questions."

"So you were here on Monday," Robert said politely but firmly.

"Look, the police have talked to me three times, and you're the second pair of kids that's been here tonight. I have a job to do, so how about leaving?"

"The second pair of kids?" My mind had latched onto that piece of information.

The cook walked toward me, spatula raised, and I stepped behind Robert. Then I stepped back out. This man really wouldn't hit me with a spatula, would he? I was willing to bet he wouldn't.

"If you would just answer one question, we'll leave," I said in a placating voice.

"What's your question?" the cook snapped, going back to scraping the grill.

"What did those two other kids look like?"

"If I answer, you'll leave?"

"Promise," I said, fighting the childish urge to cross my fingers behind my back.

"They were both about your age. The boy was probably close to six feet tall with dark, slightly curly hair, wearing a jeans jacket. The girl had shoulder-length blonde curly hair, real pretty, sort of clung to the guy. That's all I know. Now get out of here before I call the manager."

He didn't have to tell me to leave; I was already on my way. Robert was right behind me, looking somewhat puzzled.

The cook at Duffy's Tavern had just given a perfect description of Tony and Cyndee.

Chapter 19

"No. This is my problem. I'll solve it."

"Cath, why is this *your* problem?" Robert was arguing with me as we drove back to the apartment complex.

"Tony is always my problem," I answered. I was trying to figure out why I was so angry. In part, I was confused. Why were Tony and Cyndee asking questions? I knew why Robert and I were—his need for answers and my friendship with Mary explained our interest. Still, confused didn't feel like this. Maybe, I had to admit, I was jealous. Why was Tony pursuing this with Cyndee rather than me? He knew I had talked to the police and to Mary—why didn't he come to me for answers? This was different from jealousy, though. That was a sinking, sad feeling; this was harder, stronger.

Finally I figured it out. It was anger, yes, but it was anger mixed with a big dose of fear. Had Tony been mixed up in Mark's death? Suddenly I was afraid that explained Tony's appearance at the back door of Duffy's Tavern. He needed to know what the cook knew—needed to know for his own self-interest.

I was scared for Tony. There was a part of him—

a large part—that was good and caring and sensitive. That was what I loved about him. Sometimes he understood me perfectly, knowing when I needed someone to listen and when I simply needed a hug or a shoulder to cry on. Still, there was another side of Tony that had always scared me, the part that just didn't really care about much of anything. He didn't like his parents or school, and he didn't have dreams for a happy future. Still, that had been back in tenth grade. I had figured that he'd moved beyond that by now. He certainly had seemed happier, more sociable at school.

What had Tony done? Had he made some stupid mistake? I only knew I had to find out.

"Thanks for the ride," I said to Robert as he pulled up in front of my apartment. I was out of the car and up to the door of the building before he caught up with me.

"Cath, wait. What are you going to do?"

"Talk to Tony."

"How?"

"What do you mean, how?" I was losing patience with Robert. I knew it wasn't fair, but all I could think about was Tony.

"How are you going to find him?"

"Oh." Finally Robert's rational voice cut through to my brain. Tony had been with Cyndee earlier. Where was he now?

"Do you want me to go with you to look for him?" Robert asked. "Do you want me to try to find him and send him to you?"

"No," I said quietly. I wanted to talk to Tony, but I needed to find him myself, and I needed to talk to him alone. I needed to make him be honest with me, and that might take some doing. "I'll wait until tomorrow," I said.

Robert came in with me after we'd walked to the second floor and I'd unlocked the door. We talked for a while of possibilities, of what to do next, but my heart wasn't in it. The next step was Tony. Before long, we both were yawning, and I didn't argue when Robert decided to go home. I went to bed, wanting only for the hours to pass quickly between now and when I could talk to Tony.

The next morning I got up at 7:00, keyed up and anxious. I knew that I had hours to wait before I could call Tony's house on a Sunday morning, but I couldn't sleep. I tried reading, but I couldn't concentrate; I couldn't even stay curled up in bed, which is something I usually love to do. I prowled around the apartment, looking in the refrigerator ten times, looking out the windows twenty times, accomplishing absolutely nothing.

By 9:00 I was trembling, poised at the phone on the kitchen wall. I remembered Tony's number; I remembered a lot when it came to Tony. The first time I dialed his number I slammed down the receiver before I dialed the last digit. What was I going to say? What right did I have to ask him anything? Five more minutes of pacing, however, convinced me that I was going to get nothing accomplished for the rest of the day, possibly for the rest of my life, if I didn't talk to Tony.

I stomped back to the kitchen and punched the seven numbers. The ringing seemed to go on forever. Finally, on the seventh ring, a grumpy-sounding voice rasped hello.

"Hello," I said. "May I please speak to Tony?"

"Catherine, what do you want at this hour of the morning?" I hadn't recognized that particular growl as Tony's.

"It's after nine," I said, but then I realized that

had nothing to do with the point. "Tony, I need to talk to you." Silence greeted that, and I was afraid he was going to say no. "Please," I said quietly. "I wouldn't ask if it weren't important."

"Right now?" Tony asked.

"Is there any chance you could meet me in the park sometime today?" The park was where Tony and I had spent some of our best times together. Maybe it would help now.

"In an hour?" Tony asked.

"Fine," I said. "Bye." I hung up before he could change his mind—or ask any questions. I realized I hadn't told him where I'd be in the park, but I also knew he'd know right where to find me. There were some rocks along the creek at one place pretty far away from where most people went. That's where Tony had taught me how to skip rocks; that was also where we'd argued one day when he was drunk. What would this time bring?

I went to the door to retrieve the morning paper. The weather forecast in the little box in the upper right corner of the front page said it was supposed to be 50 and sunny, which wasn't bad for October. I put on jeans with heavy socks and Reeboks, then layered on a T-shirt, a turtleneck, and a sweater. That should keep me warm enough. I paced for a while longer, trying to figure out the right words to use with Tony. I must have walked miles right inside the apartment.

It was a relief when it was time to leave for the park. The rumble of the VW's engine jarred my teeth, yet I welcomed the motion. I parked in the upper lot of the park, then walked to the familiar rocks. I'd avoided that place since Tony and I had broken up, never able to separate it from all the memories. I sat on the rocks, my arms encircling my drawn-up knees, staring at the swiftly flowing water.

"Where are you, Catherine?" Tony's voice was soft in my ear, and I jumped. I hadn't heard his footsteps. "What invisible dreams are you seeing right now?"

"Just the water," I said. I moved slightly on the rock so that Tony could sit down next to me. Now that I had him here, my courage deserted me, and I didn't want to say a word.

"Catherine, what is it? You know you can tell me anything." Tony put his arm around my shoulders and squeezed.

"It's not what I want to tell you," I said. "It's what I want to ask."

"Go ahead. Ask." Tony waited through my silence until finally I began to speak.

"Tony, Robert and I talked to the cook at Duffy's Tavern." I wanted to stop right there but I couldn't, so I rushed through the next words. "He described two people who had been there earlier asking questions, and it sounded exactly like you and Cyndee." There. The words were said now; there was no going back.

"So?" Tony said. His matter-of-fact tone took away my last hope that the cook had seen two other people who just happened to look like Tony and Cyndee. So much for coincidences.

"Why, Tony?"

"Probably for the same reasons as you and Robert," Tony answered.

"I doubt that," I said sharply. Tony raised his eyebrows as he looked at me. "I somehow don't think Cyndee is overly concerned about Mary," I explained.

"And Robert is?" Tony asked.

"That's different," I said quickly.

"Why's that?" Tony questioned.

"Because Robert knows what it's like to have someone killed and never know who did it. That makes him want to find answers."

"Right, Catherine," Tony said sarcastically.

"What's that tone of voice for?" I asked, getting aggravated.

"Robert's interest has nothing to do with you?" Tony said.

"What about me?"

"Don't play dumb, Catherine. It doesn't suit you."

"Tony, Robert is my friend. He's concerned because this situation hits pretty close to home for him."

"Right," Tony said snidely. "That's why he happened to live in your apartment, and that's why he's with you all the time?"

"He doesn't live in my apartment. He's my friend," I repeated, "and I'm grateful I've gotten a second chance with him. We were all pretty brutal to him last year."

"Then what's the problem?" Tony asked. "Robert is your friend, and Cyndee is my friend."

"Right," I said in the same sarcastic tone that he had used.

"What's wrong, Catherine? Don't you believe in friendship?" Tony asked, the picture of innocence.

"Of course I do," I said, "just not you and Cyndee."

"Why not?"

"I've seen the way she looks at you, the way she drapes herself all over you. That's not the way friends act."

"Cyndee's just . . . affectionate." Even Tony had

to laugh. "Just like I am," he said, throwing both arms around me. I lost my balance and fell backward off the rocks. It was only about a three-foot drop, but I landed hard, Tony on top of me. Tony rolled off, then propped himself up on his hands and looked down at me.

"Are you okay?" he asked.

"I'm not sure," I said. I was jarred, but nothing felt broken. "Are you okay?"

"I'm fine, but you cushioned me."

"Great," I said, shifting slightly.

"Shall I kiss you and make it better?" Tony asked softly. I looked up at him, staring into his dark eyes. This was not turning out at all like I had planned.

"I need to move, please."

Tony rolled further away, and I sat up, rubbing my back.

"Let me," Tony said, starting up my shoulders and then massaging the rest of the way down.

I knew I should get back to the questions that I had come here to get answers to, but somehow I couldn't. It was much nicer to just sit here in silence, feeling Tony's hands warm and strong against my back.

Chapter 20

It was nice being close to Tony. We had decided to go for a walk, scuffing through the fallen leaves that littered the path along the creek. The air was crisp, yet without the bitter edge that another month would bring, the company was good, and the park had never seemed more tranquil. Still, I just couldn't let it be.

"Tony . . ."

"I knew this was too good to be true," he said with a laugh. "With any other girl, I could just go for a walk, relax, not think about anything serious. But this isn't just any girl. No, this is Catherine."

"And don't you forget it," I said, trying to keep the tone light, yet knowing that wouldn't last for long. "Tony . . ."

"Just don't ask," he said quietly.

"I have to," I said. "What's going on? Is there any connection at all between you and Mark's death?"

"Catherine, I may not be perfect, but I'm not a murderer."

"I know that, but I still think it's strange that you went so far as to go to Duffy's Tavern to ask questions. That isn't like you."

"What are you saying—that it's not like me to care when one of my best friends gets killed?" Sure enough, anger was starting to build in his voice.

"Care, yes. Go ask questions, get involved, no."

"I never saw you as the Nancy Drew type, either," Tony snapped.

"You know perfectly well what good friends Mary and I are," I said, my own edginess matching his.

"And this is what you try to do for your friends—solve all their problems?" Tony said sharply.

"If I can," I answered softly. "I try."

There was a long, tense silence before Tony spoke. "I'm sorry, Catherine. You didn't deserve that. I of all people should know how much you try to help those you care for."

"I'd rather have an explanation than an apology," I said, holding on to my determination.

"Catherine, there are some things I really can't explain to you. Just remember it wasn't necessarily my idea."

I didn't need any further details. "Fine, Tony," I said. "If your loyalty to Cyndee is deeper than your loyalty to me, then just forget it. I'm sorry I ever asked." I abruptly turned around and headed away from Tony. All I wanted to do was to get back to my car and escape. I had been right all along. I couldn't deal with Tony. Every time I tried, I just ended up hurt or angry.

"Catherine, stop. Listen to me." I took off running, trying to get away from the sound of his voice. Nothing made sense to me anymore, not Mark's death, not Tony, not myself. I didn't want to hear another word.

At first I heard Tony pursuing me, but I kept running until my lungs burned and my legs ached.

Soon I was back at the rocks, then up the hill to the parking area. I never looked back, never checked to see if Tony was still behind me.

My breath was coming in ragged gasps as I unlocked the VW's door and threw myself into the familiar bucket seat. The sagging springs poked me, but I didn't care. I put the key in the ignition and turned it, not even giving the engine a chance to warm up before I put it in gear and pulled away.

How stupid are you? I asked myself as I drove. What is it about you that lets you turn to Tony over and over again? What is this mysterious power that he has?

Let him go, I lectured myself. Let him go.

The trip home was a blur, my mind racing with a thousand jumbled thoughts. When I got back to the apartment complex, the parking spaces in front of my entrance were filled, and I parked on the other side of the street, relieved to be home where I could try to start to sort out the emotions that were tormenting me. I turned off the engine, got out of the car, locked the door, and started to walk, my mind back somewhere in the park with Tony. I vaguely remember looking to the right and left before I started across the drive, and I know there weren't any cars moving in my vicinity. Suddenly, though, two things happened at once. I heard a car engine gun to my left, rapidly accelerating, and I heard a voice scream "Catherine."

I turned toward the voice, leaping back as the car bore down on me. I didn't have time to run, didn't have time to think before it was upon me. That move, though, that turning toward the voice was just enough to keep me clear. I actually felt the front side of the bumper against my leg, felt the metal a fraction of an inch away. The car was dark, maybe

127

blue, and the figure behind the wheel had on a sweat shirt with the hood up, obscuring any look I might have gotten at a face. With a squeal of tires, the car sped around the first corner and was gone. A tiny part of my mind knew that I should try to see the license plate, but the rest of me shut down and stopped doing anything logical.

"Catherine, are you okay?" Tony's voice seemed to be far away. Vaguely I wondered what he was doing here. "Can you walk?"

I stared at him blankly, not knowing the answer to either of his questions. I felt his arm encircle my waist, felt him urging me forward.

"Come on, Catherine. I need to get you inside."

Inside. That was good. I knew I didn't want to be anywhere near cars. I turned myself over to Tony, letting him steer me, not really knowing where we were. The steps were familiar, but I stood motionless in front of my door until Tony took the keys out of my hand and unlocked it. I was vaguely aware that there was a piece of paper taped to the door that Tony ripped off, but I couldn't concentrate on that. Something happened to me as soon as the door shut behind us and I was in the familiar surroundings of the apartment, and I started shaking. Maybe that's when I started to realize how close that car had been. Tony put his arms around me, but even that didn't stop the shaking. My teeth were chattering as if I were freezing cold. I didn't even put my arms around him; I just stood there with my arms at my side, shaking, my mind still frozen but with flashes of images beginning to jolt through.

"Catherine, let's sit down." Tony's voice was gentle as he walked me over to the sofa. He sat down and pulled me down beside him. I curled up in a ball, my knees tucked up, and buried my face against his chest.

"It's okay," he said softly, stroking my hair. "You're okay. You're safe now. I've got you." He held me tightly, hands and voice soothing me, calming me. Still I shook. Slowly more and more of my mind was starting to function, and I didn't like the thoughts, the memory of that car. It had to have been deliberate. No, I wasn't ready to think about that, not yet.

Still Tony held me, seeming to try to stop my shaking by holding me against him as tightly as possible. I thought that if he let go, I would shake myself to pieces, and I put my arms around his neck and burrowed even closer into his chest.

"It's okay, Catherine, it's okay. I'm not going to leave you. You're safe now. I've got you. Nothing's going to hurt you." Tony murmured to me as if I were a frightened animal, calming me, reassuring me. His words kept on, but I couldn't really focus on them, could only hang on to the sound, the gentle repetition. Don't let go, I begged him, but I couldn't say the words, could only hold on tighter.

Finally, after a long time, I stopped shaking. Slowly, clearly, the questions began. "Tony," I said softly, my voice muffled because I still didn't want to lift my head from where it was buried.

"She speaks," Tony said. "I was beginning to wonder."

"Why were you here? I mean, I'm sure glad you were, but why?"

"I felt bad about the way things went in the park. Once I thought about what I'd said to you, I knew that you were right to be mad. It didn't come out the way I meant it to, and I wanted to straighten it out with you. I caught up with you a few blocks from your apartment, and had just parked when I saw that car coming at you."

"Who was it?" Suddenly that question had emerged and needed an answer.

"I don't know. All I saw was that it was heading right for you, and I screamed your name. After that all I could think about was whether you were all right. Did you see the driver?"

I stopped to think, to study whatever fragments of memory I might have. "No," I finally had to admit. "The driver had a sweat shirt on with a hood, and the hood was deep enough to hide the face. I think the car was dark blue, but that's about all that registered."

"A fine pair of detectives we'd make," Tony said, and I had to agree.

"Do you think it was just an accident, somebody leaving in a rush who didn't see me?" I asked, wanting to be reassured but knowing even as I spoke that I wouldn't believe such a reassurance.

"I'd like to believe that," Tony said softly, "but I'm afraid I doubt it." He stopped there, and I could sense his hesitation. More and more fragments of the past were beginning to filter back in.

"What was on the door?" I asked.

"Catherine, you've dealt with enough right now. Why don't you just rest?"

I lifted my head and met his eyes. Then I looked away from him and toward the coffee table. A piece of paper was laying there. I reached back and picked it up. Large letters glared at me, just like the ones on the note that had been left in my locker.

THIS IS YOUR LAST WARNING—STOP
ASKING QUESTIONS

Suddenly I wished I had listened to Tony. I dropped the paper as if it were burning my hand, and I started to shake again. Once again I wanted nothing but to be sheltered by Tony, and once again he held me tight. This time, though, what eventually stopped the shaking was the first feeling of anger.

"It's not fair," I finally said.

"What isn't?" Tony asked.

"I didn't even have a chance to stop asking questions before I was almost killed. That's not fair."

"The famous Catherine Berry sense of justice," Tony said. "I'm sorry to tell you this, but not everyone plays the game by your rules."

"I don't like this game," I said.

"Sorry, Catherine. That wasn't a very good way to say that. This goes far beyond a game."

"What happens next?" I asked. I was losing all perspective on this. It seemed like the whole world was out of balance, out of control.

"I'm not sure," Tony admitted. "Do you want to call the police?"

For a moment, that seemed tempting. Maybe Detective Martin could put all of these pieces into some kind of order. On the other hand, would he take me seriously? What proof did I have that the driver of the car had deliberately tried to hit me? I wanted help, but I wasn't sure if the police could provide it. "I don't think so," I finally said. "I couldn't stand it if they didn't take me seriously."

"Catherine, while I've been sitting here with you, I've started to figure out a few things. I don't know if I have any answers, but suddenly I know a few questions that need to be answered. Will you trust me enough to give me a few days to try to ask those questions?''

''What are they? Who can answer them?'' My curiosity was immediately fueled by Tony's statement.

''You're not going to like this, but I'm not going to tell you.''

''Tony,'' I immediately protested. ''I think I deserve to know.''

''I'm sorry, Catherine, but there is no way that I am going to see you in any more danger. You can be mad at me if you want to, but I'm not going to tell you, not yet. If I find out anything, you'll be the first to know.''

''Tony,'' I said again, ready to mount another protest.

''I couldn't stand it if anything happened to you,'' he said. ''This was too close. I need for you to be safe.'' Something in his voice made me realize that it would be useless to fuss. Besides, suddenly exhaustion hit me. I guess my adrenaline rush had finally faded, and everything was now just too much effort. I couldn't argue, and I couldn't demand; in fact, I couldn't even speak any more. My mind shut down again, and I curled against Tony. I knew that I should tell him that I was okay, that he probably had places to go and that I would be fine without him, but I didn't really want to say those words, so I didn't.

Chapter 21

I couldn't believe that I actually fell asleep, but that's what I did. I guess maybe it was some kind of protective mechanism that stopped me from freaking out or something. Anyway, when I woke up, Tony was half-sitting, half-lying on the sofa, and I was curled up beside him. His arm was over my waist, his hand warm against my stomach. I lay quietly for a moment, not wanting to wake up, knowing that I wouldn't like the realities I'd have to face. Still, I had to move. My back hurt, and I had to go to the bathroom.

I moved slightly, and Tony's arm tightened around me. "You're okay," he said.

"Thanks to you," I answered.

"I'm glad I was here," he said, leaning down to kiss the top of my head.

"What if you hadn't . . ."

"Stop, Catherine," Tony interrupted. "You'll drive yourself crazy with 'what if's.' I was there and you're safe and that's all that matters."

I sat up, not wanting to leave the nest of warmth beside Tony but knowing I had to. I got up and walked to the bathroom, looking back at Tony and giving him the best smile I could manage. Seeing my face in the mirror did nothing to restore my confidence. I was extremely pale, and my eyes looked bigger than usual. My hair was a mess, and I raked my fingers through it without much success before I went back out to Tony.

He was sitting on the sofa looking at the sheet of paper that had been taped to the door. He quickly put it back on the table when he saw me, but I went over and picked it up again. Then I went to my room and got the first note out of my desk drawer and brought it out with me.

I sat down beside Tony and held out both notes. "Sure looks like they're from the same person," I said. Granted both were in heavy block letters, but they were done in the same style, the same black ink.

"You're amazing," Tony said.

"Why?" I asked.

"You were almost killed today, and now you're right back at this. I've always admired your strength, and this sure proves it."

"Strong? Tony, a little while ago I was shaking and in shock. That's not a very strong reaction."

"You're human, Catherine. You're allowed to be scared. It's just that you don't give in to it for very long."

"I'd feel even better if you'd tell me about those ideas of yours."

"No way, Catherine. Don't even try. You're not going to sweet talk that out of me. I told you—no more risks."

"I seem to be at risk no matter what I do," I said. "Maybe if you tell me what you know, it'll be over faster. Maybe there's something I can do to help."

"Catherine, trust me. Give me two days. That's all I ask."

I didn't like the thoughts that were pouring into my head, thoughts that I wanted to drive out but couldn't. My silence must have given Tony some idea of what I was thinking.

"I know I haven't given you much reason to trust me," he said. "I've done some pretty stupid things, and unfortunately the most stupid ones have involved you."

I wondered what he was thinking of. Probably the time he drove my car drunk and then had me switch seats with him so the policeman who stopped us wouldn't know he had been drinking. That was what had led me to break up with him. Then there was his flaunting of other girls, Cyndee among them. He had always claimed that I was different from the rest, but I was afraid to believe him.

"I want you to know that right now I'm not playing games. The stakes are too high. I'll do whatever I can to see that you're safe," Tony continued.

"I believe that," I said. Even when things were at their worst, I knew that I had never wished any harm to Tony, and I believed he felt the same about me.

"Two days," Tony said. "If I haven't figured anything out by Tuesday night, I'll tell you everything I've been thinking, or I'll go to Detective Martin with you or whatever you choose. Is it a deal?"

I thought about it, but I couldn't see any alternatives. I couldn't force information out of Tony, and I didn't want to go to the police myself without stronger evidence. "Okay," I said reluctantly.

With that, the doorbell rang. I jumped at the

sound, still more tense than I had realized. What if it was the person who had left the note? It didn't make sense to come back and ring the doorbell, but then what had been making sense lately?

"I'll get it," Tony said. He got up and walked to the door. I stayed on the sofa for a moment, but then I couldn't bear not to know. I was about ten steps away when I heard Tony, open the door and heard a welcome, familiar voice.

"Hello," Robert said. "I came to see if Cath had any news."

"Well, I'm not sure . . ." Before Tony could finish, I got to the door.

"Robert! You won't believe what happened." I knew that he was wondering what I'd found out from Tony, but that was rather awkward to discuss at the moment. I glanced at Tony and saw that he didn't look too pleased. Still, Robert had been involved in this from the start, and there was no way I wasn't going to tell him what had happened.

The three of us walked back to the living room, and Tony and Robert stood there rather awkwardly. I sat down in the chair, leaving the sofa to the two of them. Robert sat, but Tony still stood, looking first at me and then at Robert.

"I guess I'd better get going," Tony said.

"Don't let me interrupt," said Robert, starting to get up.

"Don't be silly," I said, and Robert sat down again.

"I have some things that need to be done," Tony said. I didn't really want him to leave, but if he was going to find out anything that would help settle this whole mess, then he would have to.

Tony looked at Robert, seeming to hesitate before

he spoke again. "Look after Catherine," he finally said. "Make sure she stays here."

"Tony, don't talk about me as if I'm some kind of patient," I said with a laugh. "I'm okay."

"I'm not so sure about that," Tony said. Meanwhile, Robert was looking from one of us to the other, thoroughly confused.

"I'll walk you out," I said to Tony. Robert would just have to stay confused for a couple more minutes.

Tony and I walked down the steps toward the front door of the building. When Tony was at the bottom and I was on the first step, he stopped abruptly, turning around so that I stopped, too.

"I don't want you going out into the parking lot," he said. I had been ready to walk outside with him, but he was right. Suddenly I didn't want to set foot in that parking lot again.

"That's going to make it kind of hard to lead a normal life," I said, trying to lighten the mood. "I mean, how am I going to get to my car or go to school or anything if I can't cross the driveway?"

"Maybe you'd better not go to school for a couple of days," Tony said quietly.

His concern was starting to unnerve me. "Tony, I'm scared, I admit, but I'm not going to be a prisoner in my own home. I can't stop living because some crazy person thinks I ask too many questions."

Tony reached up to me, encircling me with his arms. It felt weird. Because I was up one step, our heights were equalized and I could meet his eyes straight on rather than having to look up at him.

"Catherine, I don't want anything to happen to you. You matter to me." He hugged me tightly against him. "I need for you to be safe."

Tony had succeeded in chasing away any protests I might have launched.

"So this is what it would be like to kiss you if you were taller," Tony finally said lightly. "You're one step short."

I stepped down to his level, and once again my head nestled under his chin.

"One step short, am I?" I said. I climbed up two steps, where I was taller than him. The only problem was that now I had to lean across to him, almost losing my balance.

"Definitely only one step short," Tony said. "Come here." I went back down to the landing, and he put one hand under my chin, tilting my face up to meet his eyes. "Lock the door behind you," he said.

I went back up to the very confused Robert. Just as I was about to start the story, the phone rang. What now, I thought. Half-fearing it was my father, I answered it. Mary's voice was welcome, and I promptly invited her over. That way I could tell the saga to both of them at once. Poor Robert waited impatiently for Mary.

I'm glad I told them both together, because it shook me up again to relive it in words. Mary ended up more upset than I was, and Robert had to calm both of us down. Finally we settled in to brainstorming, thinking of any possible people who could have been in that car. All we did, though, was get more confused. If there were answers, I couldn't find them. I only hoped that Tony was having more success.

Finally I decided that our brains were not functioning clearly because of hunger, and I suggested going out for pizza.

"How about if we have it delivered?" Robert asked. Mary quickly agreed.

"Look, guys, I appreciate your concern, but I'm not going to stay cooped up in here forever. I think that we would be safe going out for pizza," I said.

"Tony said to keep you here," Robert said.

"He just meant he didn't want me out alone," I said. "Come on." I got up and headed decisively for the door. Robert and Mary scrambled after me, making me laugh.

I have to admit that I looked both ways about four times before we crossed the driveway to Mary's car, and Robert and Mary stood real close on either side of me. When we sprinted across, they actually had me by either arm. Anybody who saw us must have thought we were crazy.

To be honest, I really didn't enjoy the pizza. The whole time we were driving, I kept looking for that car, and the whole time we were eating, I kept looking at the people, wondering.

No wonder Robert had such a hard time after his father's death, I realized. It's horrible to have every stranger suddenly become a suspect. It's even worse when people you know are suspects, too.

Chapter 22

The next two days at school were bizarre. Mary insisted on borrowing her mother's car and picking me up and taking me home, and every time I turned around either she or Robert was at my side. I swear they must have set up a schedule of who met me after which class. Other than that, I kept a low profile. I didn't talk to anybody, and I sure didn't ask any questions.

I only saw Tony briefly. I tried to question him about what he was doing, but he brushed me off with a sudden desire to get to class on time. Cyndee was still definitely around him, which left me as confused as ever. I mattered to him, but he spent much more time with her. Who could understand Tony? All I knew was that the first mystery to be solved involved Mark's death and the source of my warnings; when that was done, just maybe I'd work on figuring out Tony. He was enough of a puzzle to last me a lifetime.

By the end of the school day on Tuesday, I was getting impatient. Tony had asked for two days, and his time was just about up. I walked out of my last class of the day ready to find him and force some kind of decision. If he didn't have a plan, I would have to go to Detective Martin, much as I feared that he wouldn't take me seriously. I was shoving books in my locker, waiting for Mary, who I knew would catch up with me there, when Tony walked down the hallway toward me. Good, I thought. That saves me a phone call.

"So what have you found out?" I asked as soon as he was in voice range.

"I'm just not sure yet," Tony said, coming to stand next to me. "I think I need some more time."

"Tony, you promised. Two days. That was our deal. I can't keep on like this." I had thought I was pretty calm, but I guess the tension was catching up to me.

"Okay," Tony said, with definite reluctance in his voice. "After all I've done to you, I can't expect you to take my word for anything. You deserve proof, and I've been trying to find a way to get it for you. I need to have a conversation with someone else in your presence. I don't guarantee this will work, and I don't feel good about doing it, but it's the only thing I can think of."

"Fine. Where shall we meet?" Any move was better than this.

"It's a little more complicated than that. The other person can't know you're listening."

I was getting more confused by the minute, but I knew better than to ask too many questions. I didn't want to give Tony any excuses to back down. "How about if I hide in the backseat of a car or something?" I asked, desperately fishing around in my mind for a possibility.

"I don't quite think that would work, Catherine."

"How about our apartment?" I asked. "My mother and Mr. Donelly are still in Ireland."

"No, that won't work, either. It can't be your place."

Of course, I was trying to figure out who this mysterious person was with whom Tony needed to talk. If my apartment wouldn't do, maybe that meant it was someone who knew me. There. That sure helped, I thought sarcastically. "How about Robert's apartment?" I asked.

"He has his own place?" Tony asked.

"It's in the same complex as mine," I said, forgetting how little Tony really knew about Robert.

"How convenient," Tony said.

"Stop that," I said. "Will his apartment do?"

"Will he let us use it?"

"I'm sure he will if it means getting information to end this whole mess," I said.

"Well, I don't like it, but I can't think of any other possibilities. Tell him to leave a key on the ledge over the door. I'll be there around eight o'clock. Is there a place where you can hear yet be out of sight?"

"If I stay in the bedroom with the door shut all but a crack, I should be able to hear whatever goes on in the living room," I said.

"Catherine, do you promise not to get involved, no matter what you hear? I need to do this myself."

"I promise," I said, not positive it was a promise I could keep. Mary was turning the corner toward me, so I quickly told Tony where Robert's apartment was. He wheeled away before Mary got to us.

"I see Tony's in a sociable mood," Mary said. "What's his problem?" I was silent for a moment, debating. Should I tell her about Tony's plan for tonight? Tony had not specifically said that I couldn't tell anyone, yet I was pretty certain he wouldn't want others to know. Still, I was sick of secrecy. Mary and I had been through enough lately, and I didn't want to start going behind her back. I told her about the plan.

"I want to be there, too," was Mary's immediate reaction.

"I don't think that's a good idea," I said quickly. "Tony didn't say anything about others being there."

"Cath, it was my boyfriend who was killed."

"I'm not forgetting that," I said. "I'll tell you what. Why don't you wait at my apartment, and the second I can, I'll come tell you what happened."

"Sorry, Cath. Not good enough."

I knew that I wasn't going to convince Mary otherwise, and in a way I didn't blame her. If there were answers, she needed to hear them, too.

"What about Robert?" I asked. "We have to convince him to let us use the apartment."

"He should be there, too." Mary sounded absolutely settled on that.

"Mary, we can't exactly have a party there. Next you'll want to invite the whole senior class."

"Just the three of us," Mary said. "You two are the ones who have been there for me through all of this, and I want you both there. Now who do you think Tony is bringing?" With that, Mary was off and running with a string of ideas. I didn't even try to stop her, and she didn't notice my silence as she drove home.

I picked up the mail, checked the door for more notes, went in and dumped my books in my room, and then Mary and I walked over to Robert's to tell him about tonight's plan. He immediately agreed to the use of his apartment, looking around in mock horror.

"Oh no, guests already, and my decorator just

hasn't had time to finish." Mary and I both laughed; if anything, the apartment looked worse now than it had before he moved in, and that was saying something. Robert also immediately agreed with Mary that he should be there. It would have been hard to say no; after all, it was his apartment.

We ran a few trial runs with one of us talking at a normal volume in the living room while the other two hid behind the bedroom door. As long as the door was left open at least a fraction of an inch, we thought we'd be able to hear. Then we checked to see whether we would be visible either in the crack at the side or under the door. Unless Tony's mystery person was flat on the floor, we figured we were safe.

Robert decided that it might be better if his car was out of sight, and Mary and I agreed even though we couldn't figure out quite why. We rode with him while he parked it near my building, and then we all three gathered in my apartment. Our nervousness showed; every conversation faded out after a few sentences, and we were all having trouble finding new topics. We had given up even guessing what Tony was up to, and nothing else really mattered.

Finally, in desperation, I suggested that we bake cookies. Mary and Robert looked at me as if I were crazy, but they agreed. I managed to scrape together the ingredients for chocolate chip cookies—we had a bag of chips, butter, flour, brown sugar, eggs, milk, and vanilla.

The first obstacle was that the butter needed to be softened.

"I think my mother said you can soften butter in the microwave," Mary said.

"Good thinking," I said. "How long?"

"I don't know, about a minute, I guess," Mary said.

"What about the paper?" I asked, looking dubiously at the stick of butter I was holding.

"No problem. My mom cooks things on paper towels all the time, and that's sort of the same." Mary was turning into a veritable fountain of cooking information.

I opened the door of the microwave and put in the stick of butter, paper and all. "A minute?" I asked Mary to be sure.

"Yeah, sounds good. If it's not soft enough, we can do it longer."

I set the timer and pushed start. "Keep an eye on that, Robert," I said, since he was standing back being of no help at all. He came closer to the microwave, and Mary and I started to crack the eggs into a mixing bowl.

The timer had not yet rung on the microwave when Robert spoke. "Cath, I think you'd better come check this."

"Just a second," I said, in the middle of picking out some pieces of eggshell that had accidentally fallen in.

"I think you'd better check this real soon," Robert said.

I gave up on the eggshells and walked over to the microwave just as the timer rang. Punching the door release button, I stared in horror. The butter was a golden puddle in the bottom of the microwave, the paper a flat, greasy rectangle. As I watched, the butter began to flow out of the bottom and onto the counter.

"Mary," I said quietly. "Mary," I then repeated with rising volume. "I think you were a little off with your butter theory."

"Need more time?" Mary asked from the other end of the counter, busily measuring sugar.

"Not quite," I said. "Get over here."

"What's your problem, Cath?" she asked, throwing down the sugar scoop. When she got to the microwave and looked in, though, she gasped. "Oops," she said.

"Oops?" I said. "Oops? The microwave is a sea of liquid butter, and all you can say is oops?"

I thought I heard a muffled sound from Robert's direction.

"Close the door. It's leaking out," was Mary's only contribution.

I slammed the door shut, and then Mary and I stared at each other. "Maybe it was fifteen seconds," Mary said with a puzzled look.

"Now you tell me," I said.

"Look, it's just a stick of butter. Get out another one."

"That was the last one," I said. "Besides, who is going to clean up that mess?"

"Robert," Mary said sweetly.

"Why me?" Robert asked.

"Because you were supposed to keep an eye on it," Mary retorted.

"It just went so fast," Robert said seriously. "One second it looked fine, and the next second, it sort of collapsed and liquified."

Suddenly the whole thing struck me as funny. Who ever heard of butter collapsing? I started to laugh, and within seconds Mary was laughing with me. Robert looked at us in amazement. I laughed until tears were running down my face.

"Now what do we do?" I asked. "We've cracked the eggs, and they'll go to waste if we don't bake these cookies."

"I'll go buy more butter," Robert volunteered, probably to get away from this lunacy.

"That will take too long," I said. "Let's try to salvage the butter."

"How?" Mary asked. "It's trying to escape." We both looked at the pool on the counter.

"I know," I said. I got out a rubber spatula and a long, flat tray. "Open the door and put this tray at the edge real fast, and then scoot the butter out of the microwave."

Mary and Robert looked rather dubious, but I gave them no chance to argue. I shoved the tray into Robert's hands, and put Mary in charge of the spatula. "Ready?" I asked.

"Go for it," Mary said. I opened the door, and a little of the butter immediately headed for the counter.

"Catch it," I yelled to Robert, and he got the tray in place. Mary reached in and picked up the paper as if it was a dead animal or something. She dropped it on the tray, and then began to guide the liquid butter out of the microwave. I went back to measuring.

"Maybe if we put this melted butter in the freezer, it would end up right," I heard Mary suggest.

"I've had about enough of your butter theories," I said. "What do you think will happen if we just use it like it is?"

Nobody had any answers, so we decided to try it. The cookies were okay, but a little weird. They all ran together and had to be cut apart with a knife, but other than the tray that burned because Robert forgot to watch it, they were definitely edible. Mary and I forced Robert to wash up the bowls and spoons and trays as punishment for his inept watching performances. We all gorged on cookies, ending up too full to consider a real dinner.

Ultimately, the cookies didn't matter at all. A glance at the clock on the kitchen wall revealed that we had managed to fill three hours without a word about Tony and tonight. We had actually managed to laugh, something I would have thought impossible earlier in the day.

Finally, though, it was time to get ready. We all agreed that we needed to be back to Robert's apartment by 7:00, just in case Tony came early. Almost reluctantly, we left behind the apartment that smelled of freshly baked cookies and headed for the door. We all became silent again as we walked the blocks to Robert's apartment. Once again Robert and Mary flanked me on either side, and the seriousness of what was to come once again weighed heavy on us.

Robert unlocked his door, took his key off the ring and put it on the ledge over his door, and then relocked his door from inside. We sat in the living room for a few minutes, knowing that most likely we still had a while to wait, but at every noise we flinched, poised to hear a key in the door. After several false alarms, we decided we'd be better off in the bedroom.

I felt a little foolish as we walked into the bedroom, shut the door all but a tiny bit, and then sat down on the floor. It took us several tries before we found an arrangement that worked. I sat closest to the door, with Mary a little behind and to my left, and Robert to my right. Occasionally one of us would shift and jostle another, and we would apologize in a whisper, then realize that we really didn't need to whisper yet. The tension built with every passing moment, every noise in the hallway, every car engine. It was dark outside now, and even though we had left on a light in the living room, we couldn't see. I wanted something to happen, anything to happen to end this waiting.

Chapter 23

A combination of fear and relief swept through me when I finally heard a key in the door. Although I knew that we were out of sight, I was suddenly convinced that whoever was with Tony would immediately know that we were behind the door. I was holding my breath without even realizing it. The door shut, and then I heard a decidedly feminine giggle. Well, that sure narrowed down the possibilities. What was Tony up to?

"Tony, what a great idea. Whose apartment is this?" I knew that voice, and I wasn't the least bit happy to hear it.

"A friend's," Tony answered vaguely.

"So why did you bring me here, as if I couldn't guess?" I hated the teasing note in Cyndee's voice. I could just imagine where her hands were about now.

"I think you've got the wrong idea," Tony said quickly.

"I doubt that," Cyndee said. "I think we've both got a fine idea." There was a moment's silence, during which my fingernails bit into my palms.

"We need to talk," Tony said, and I heard the seriousness in his voice, even if Cyndee didn't.

"You borrowed a friend's apartment so we could be alone to talk?" she asked, giggling again.

"Yes," Tony said. "I didn't want us to be interrupted."

"This sounds serious," Cyndee said, and there was a different note in her voice this time.

"It is," Tony said. "There's something I need to tell you, and I'm not sure how to do it."

"So talk," Cyndee said. "What's so hard about that?"

"It's just that I don't think you want to hear this," Tony said.

"Tony, this is boring. Get to the point." The purr had definitely gone out of Cyndee's voice.

"You know who I used to date," Tony began, and my heart began to race. What was he doing? Why on earth was he having this conversation with Cyndee? What was he trying to prove?

"I suppose you mean Cath Berry, although I never figured out just what it was you saw in her. I mean she's not exactly your type. She's always seemed sort of innocent and . . . boring, if you know what I mean. I can't see her just letting go and having fun."

"There's a lot more to Catherine than you see," Tony said. I had been wondering when he was going to get around to defending me.

"Yes, but can she show you as good a time as I can?" Cyndee asked, and I had no doubt that once again she was doing more than talking. I hated her.

"That's not the point," Tony said hurriedly. "Catherine means something to me on a level I can't quite explain. Even when I don't see her, I still feel like she's a part of my life, like there's a connection between us. I always know that if I need to, I can turn to her."

"That's real sweet," Cyndee said sarcastically. "Why are you telling me all of this?"

"I can't see you anymore," Tony said simply.

"What do you mean?" Cyndee snapped.

"I mean that I want to do everything I can to get back together with Catherine. I can't walk with you at school, or go out with you, any of that. I want to prove to Catherine that she can trust me again."

"I don't believe I'm hearing this," Cyndee snapped. "You really are a bastard, just like all the rest."

"What's that supposed to mean?" Tony asked.

"All you guys with your sweet little virginal girlfriends who come to me when you want your boring lives spiced up. I'm good enough to cheat with, but not good enough to be seen with, is that it?" Her voice was getting louder and shriller with each word.

"That's not what I meant," Tony said.

"Isn't it?" Cyndee yelled. "I think that's exactly what you mean. I'm fine to hang out with until you decide it's time to get serious, and then you go running back to little Miss Goody-Two-Shoes, the perfect girl to take home to meet Mommy and Daddy." Considering how much Tony disliked his parents, she was off target on that one.

"Now wait a minute," Tony said, anger showing in his voice for the first time. "You're the one who came after me, remember?"

"What's that supposed to mean?"

"How about that day at the mall?" Tony asked. "You and Mark were there and I ran into you, and then suddenly you were all over me."

"You have your precious Catherine to thank for that," Cyndee said snidely. "What was I supposed to do? If she saw me with Mark, she would have gone running to tell Mary, and then Mark would have been mad at me. You were . . ."

She hesitated, and Tony filled in the blank. "Convenient?"

"Well, sort of," Cyndee said. "You know how afraid Mark was that Mary would find out that he was seeing me behind her back."

I could feel Mary stiffen behind me, and I stuck a hand back to her. She grabbed it and held on.

"Mark and I agreed that it would be much safer if I was seen around school with you."

"Thanks a lot," Tony said sharply.

"Don't get me wrong," Cyndee said. "It's not that I don't like you. I do—a lot. I think we have a real good thing going. When you really think about it, you'll figure out that I'm the one you really want, not the brain of the senior class. I mean, who wants to date someone who's taking Calculus?" Even I could hear the desperate edge in Cyndee's flirtation, but I was gripping Mary's hand as hard as she was gripping mine.

"I do," Tony said quietly. "I like the fact that Catherine is smart. The fact that she thinks so much makes me think, too."

"So you're saying I'm stupid?" Cyndee asked, her voice again raising.

"No, but I am saying that I'm not going to see you again."

There was silence, and my mind raced through it. Was this all that Tony was up to? He was trying to break up with Cyndee in front of me so that I would want to go out with him again? I was suddenly humiliated at the thought that both Mary and Robert were hearing this. It should be private. I shouldn't even be overhearing this.

"You and Mark are two of a kind, aren't you?"

Cyndee's voice startled me because the words were almost hissed.

"Why?" Tony asked.

"Because that's exactly what he said to me," she said, "and I'm sick of hearing this. I'm sick of it, do you understand? I don't want to hear this. Leave me alone. Let me out of here. I hate you. I hate you all."

I couldn't figure out what was happening. Suddenly Cyndee was yelling, and I couldn't figure out where the intensity was coming from.

"Come back here," Tony said. "You can't leave yet."

"I can do any damn thing I want to," Cyndee screamed. "I hate you. Do you understand? I hate you." Her last words were twisted around sobs.

"It's okay," I heard Tony say. "It's okay. You have to talk about it. You have to. You must know that."

Cyndee's sobs grew louder and then were muffled, I guessed by Tony's shoulder.

"I can't," she finally said, her voice cracking on the words.

"You have to," Tony said, firmly yet gently. "You can't go on like this."

"I'm so scared," Cyndee said, her sobbing intensifying again.

"I know," Tony said. "I know you're scared. But you have to deal with this. It just isn't going to go away."

"It would if she would just let it alone," Cyndee said. I knew she meant me.

"This isn't Catherine's fault," Tony said. "If she weren't asking questions, someone else would."

"But she's the smart one," Cyndee said. "Make her stop."

"That's not the answer," Tony replied. "You're the one who has to stop it."

"I can't," Cyndee cried.

"You have to," Tony repeated. "You have to. This has to stop."

"For your precious Catherine?" Cyndee lashed out.

"For you, too," Tony replied.

"You don't care about me. Nobody does," Cyndee said.

"That's not true," Tony said. "Plenty of people care about you. But you have to tell them the truth."

"Everyone will hate me."

"I think they'll understand. Try me. Talk to me, Cyndee." I recognized that calm, soothing voice that Tony was so good at using.

"It was his fault," Cyndee said, her voice suddenly loud again. "It was his fault," she repeated, more quietly and tentatively.

"Why was it Mark's fault?" Tony asked.

"Because he made me mad. He made me feel like trash. I needed to hurt him, to make him feel as bad as I did."

"Did he tell you he couldn't see you anymore?"

"Yes," Cyndee said. "Yes."

"When you were in the car in the parking lot of Duffy's Tavern?"

"Yes," she said again. "We were in the car. He told me that he loved Mary, and that he was afraid she would find out, and he didn't want to see me anymore." Behind me I felt Mary's head lean into my back. I could feel her fist clenched against her mouth.

"And you were mad?" Tony asked quietly, as if he were afraid to interrupt her narrative.

"I was mad," she repeated in an almost childlike

voice. "He hurt me. He made me feel like someone not good enough, not clean enough, and I hated him right then."

Tony waited through a silence, then prodded again. "So you yelled at him?"

"Yes," Cyndee said. "I had turned off the car, and we were sitting talking, and he told me that, and I wanted him out of the car, out of the car if I wasn't good enough for him. I wanted him away from me."

"So what did you do?" Tony asked. "You wanted Mark away from you, so what did you do?"

"I screamed at him to get out, and he said for me just to take him home, and I didn't want to because I wasn't the one he wanted anyway, I wasn't good enough for him, so I reached across him to the door handle and I threw open the door and I shoved him." Cyndee's voice was almost trancelike, suddenly flat and emotionless. "I tried to shove him out of the car because I wasn't good enough for him. I shoved him and hit him until he fell out of the car to get away from me, and I looked at him laying on the ground. I guess he hit his head but I didn't care. I was glad that he was on the ground and that he was dirty, because he thought that I was dirty."

"You could see him on the ground?" Tony asked.

"I could see him," Cyndee said. "He was on the ground, but he wasn't dead. He was just lying there. He wasn't dead," she said, and suddenly the flatness was replaced by the risking keen of hysteria.

"I pulled the door shut, and I started the car, and I drove away."

"Is there any way . . ."

"He wasn't dead. He wasn't. I know he wasn't. I saw him. I didn't run over him. I know I didn't.

156

I've gone over it in my head a million times, and I didn't. I remember pulling away from him, steering the other way so I wouldn't hit him. I even looked back, and I knew that he was lying there and I left real fast because I figured that any second he would get up and come after me because he'd be so mad that I hit him. I just wanted to teach him a lesson, that he couldn't treat me that way. I didn't want him to be dead." She was crying again. "You believe me, don't you?"

"Yes, I believe you," Tony said. "There's a lot of traffic in and out of there. Someone else must have hit him right after you left."

"What happens now?" Cyndee asked, her voice shaky. "Are you going to tell anybody?"

"No," Tony said, "You are."

"No," Cyndee cried out. "No, I can't."

"You told me, and I believed you. Now you have to tell the police."

"No," Cyndee wailed. "They'll put me in jail. I won't. You can't make me. I'll run away if you try to make me."

"You can't run far enough," Tony said quietly. "Cyndee, you don't have any choices. You have to tell the police what happened. This isn't a secret you can live with. It will eat you up alive."

"I thought it would be okay if Cath would just stop," Cyndee said more quietly. "I thought I could scare her."

"So you left those notes?" Tony asked.

"Yes, just to scare her," Cyndee answered.

"What about in the parking lot on Sunday?"

"That wasn't me," Cyndee said, panic filling her voice. "You can't prove anything."

"Come on, Cyndee," Tony said, his voice still calm and gentle.

"I just went to leave the note on her door," Cyndee finally said. "I called her apartment, and when nobody answered I figured it was safe to go there and leave the note real fast and then go. I even borrowed my sister's car so nobody would recognize it."

"And then Catherine came back?"

"I was just ready to pull out and I saw her and I thought I could scare her even more. Just scare her, nothing else."

"You almost hit her," Tony said.

"But I didn't," Cyndee said. "I just wanted her to leave me alone so nobody would know."

"It won't work, will it?"

"Yes," she said, desperation filling her voice. "It will work. Just don't say anything and I promise I'll never bother Cath again. Soon everybody will forget."

"It doesn't work that way," Tony said. "You'll never forget. You need help in dealing with this, and you'll never get it if you don't face up to what happened."

Suddenly Cyndee began sobbing again, and she cried and cried as if she would never stop.

"You know I'm right," Tony said after a while. "Come on. I'll take you."

"I'm scared," was all that Cyndee said.

Then there were no more words, only Cyndee's sobs and the closing of the door behind them.

Chapter 24

For a moment or two, nobody moved. Then Mary
and I turned so that we were facing each other, each
crying on the other's shoulder. I could feel Robert
patting first one of us and then the other on the
back.

"Poor Mark," Mary said. I knew that it would
take time for Mary to accept the fact that Mark had
been cheating on her; for now, all she could see was
his sad and lonely death.

What surprised me was that in my mind I was
thinking, "poor Cyndee." I had never liked the girl,
but I cried in part for her. She had been hurt and
mad, but she had never figured on causing Mark's
death. What a horrible thing to live with.

Finally I felt Robert stand up. "Let's go in the
living room," he said. It took those words to make
me realize how cramped my legs were, and I stood
up, helping Mary up in the process. Slowly the three
of us walked into the living room. The light made
my eyes hurt, and I shielded them. Mary and I stood
in the living room, still crying. I heard Robert
rattling around in the kitchen, and in a minute he
came back with glasses of water for us. I wasn't
sure what that was supposed to solve, but I took a

few sips, and so did Mary. Then we gave the glasses back to Robert, who ducked back into the kitchen.

"It's better to know," he said when he came back.

"I know," I said, fighting to regain my composure.

"Even if it hurts," Robert added, looking at Mary.

"I guess," she finally said. "It's just that I want to remember Mark as . . ."

"Perfect?" Robert said. "He wasn't. None of us are. We need to remember that."

"But what if you had found out something bad about your father?" Mary blurted out.

"I'd still rather know," Robert said without hesitation. He started talking to Mary about all that had happened to him after his father's death, telling her the story he'd already told me about the silence, the suspicion, the searching. I could see Mary lose herself in his words, and I was grateful to Robert. He was still talking quite a while later when his doorbell rang.

"I'll get it," I said quickly, not wanting him to stop.

I opened the door to see Tony's pale, shadowed face. I could see him look beyond me to Mary and Robert, but I couldn't read his reaction to seeing them.

"You go ahead," Mary said. "You two need to talk."

"Will you be okay?" I asked her, turning back to look at her face, still puffy from crying.

"Yes," she said. "I think I will."

"But your car is back at my place," I protested.

"I'll walk her back," Robert said.

I looked at Tony, and I knew that he was the one I should be worried about at the moment. We left.

"My car's at your place," Tony said quietly. "I checked there first before I came over here."

I was glad that we had a few blocks to walk. The temperature had fallen and it felt like rain; maybe the cold, damp air would help me think. We walked in silence. Back at my apartment, Tony slumped on the sofa, his head thrown back, staring up toward the ceiling.

"Did you take Cyndee to the police station?" I finally asked.

"Yes," Tony said. "Detective Martin was there, so that's who she talked to. When I left, her parents had just gotten there."

"You did the right thing," I said, reaching out to take one of his hands, lacing my fingers through his.

"That doesn't make me feel very good right now," he answered.

"How did you figure it out?" I asked.

"I think I knew all along, but I just didn't want to face it," Tony said.

"Did you know that Mark was seeing her?"

"Yes," he admitted, "and the day before he died, Mark told me that he was going to tell Cyndee it was over. He really did care about Mary in his own way."

He sure had a great way of showing it, I almost said, but then I heard Robert's words: Nobody's perfect. Remember that.

"So you knew that they had been arguing in the parking lot?"

"It seemed like a good guess, but I also couldn't believe that Cyndee would knowingly try to kill him."

"She didn't mean to," I said.

"So you believe her, too," Tony said, a statement rather than a question.

"How did you know she would talk to you?" I asked.

"I had a feeling that if I almost recreated the situation, said to her what I figured Mark must have said, that the memories would be so strong that she wouldn't be able to hide from them."

"So that's why you said what you did about me," I said quietly, nodding my head in understanding.

"No, Catherine," Tony said. "I meant everything I said. I would never have gotten involved if it weren't for you."

"Even if you had figured out what Cyndee did?"

"Even then," Tony said. "It would have been a lot easier to let someone else deal with it—unless that someone else was you."

"You did the right thing," I said.

"I believe that now," Tony said. "But I'm not sure I did it for the right reasons. I didn't really do it to help Cyndee. I did it to try to make things right again with you."

"What do you mean?" I asked quietly.

"Catherine, do you remember two nights ago when I told you that you were one step short?"

"Of course I do," I said, a slight smile crossing my face at the memory.

"I was wrong," Tony said. "I'm the one who's always one step short. I had this plan in my mind that one day everything would be perfect. I would get my life figured out, and I'd know who I was and what I wanted and then—only then—would I come back to get you. I had this image in my mind that you would be waiting for me, knowing that I'd be back to sweep you off your feet."

"What changed that?" I asked.

"Seeing you with Robert," Tony said, not meeting my eyes. "I suddenly realized that I wasn't the only one who could see how special you are, and that my life was always going to be at least one step short of being perfect. So while I was waiting around to get everything figured out and dating girls who really didn't mean anything, you weren't exactly going to be frozen in time waiting around for me."

I started to tell him that Robert and I were friends with no romance involved, but I stopped myself.

"I couldn't stand for you to be in danger, and I couldn't stand the thought of losing you," he said, then looked back at me. This time I was the one who looked away.

"I'm not exactly yours to lose," I said.

"I know that," Tony said. "I've been acting like I have all the time in the world to waste before I try to fix what's really important to me. I guess Mark's death has convinced me that we're not promised anything.

"Catherine, I want a chance to prove that you can trust me. I don't blame you if you don't right now, but I want you to know that I'm done running away. I'm done being scared of my feelings for you."

I didn't know what to say, but I knew I needed to say something. "I think you proved a lot tonight," I said.

"Do I get one more chance?" Tony asked. A tired smile crossed his face. "If I screw up this time, you can rent a billboard to put up a sign announcing to the world that Tony Richardson is a jerk. I'll even help pay for it."

"How about an airplane pulling a banner?" I asked.

"Can we compromise on a full-page ad in the newspaper?" Tony said.

"It's a deal. You've got your chance." I loosed my hand from his grip and put my arms around his neck. "Even if I am a brainy, virginal goody-goody?" I asked teasingly.

"We could change that," Tony said lightly.

"In your dreams," I snapped back, but with a smile.

"Why did I have to fall in love with a girl with principles?" Tony asked, and then he pulled me to my feet and kissed me. Actually, first he hugged me. He linked his arms tightly around me, squeezing me, then gently rubbed my back, finally settling his hands lower and pulling me even closer against him. His cheek was resting against the top of my head, and my face was tucked against him, my hands around his neck, tangled in his silky hair. Gently he raised his hands and put them under my chin, tilting it upward until my eyes met his. I looked at him, feeling his intensity, then looked away, almost frightened by what I felt. Tony kissed the top of my head, then my forehead, then, once again lifting my face, the tip of my nose. Finally, lightly, quietly, he kissed my lips once, twice, a third time. His hands again circled me, warm against my back, and the next kiss was more probing until I couldn't tell who was kissing and who was being kissed. I could no longer think, only feel. When the kiss ended, I once again put my head under his chin, feeling his heartbeat, feeling my own. We swayed gently back and forth as if dancing to silent music. Tony gave me one last hug, then bent his knees, grabbed me tightly, and lifted me into the air. I wasn't one step short anymore.

He put me down. "I'd think I'd better go," he

said, and after one more quick kiss, one last hug, he did.

Even if I didn't have the courage to tell him then, I knew that I loved him.

I couldn't change that any more than I could change the date of my birth or the color of my eyes.

Chapter 25

Four days later, I went to the Philadelphia Airport to pick up my mother and Mr. Donelly. As soon as she got through Customs, my mother threw her arms around me, hugging me fiercely.

"How are you?" she asked breathlessly. "I missed you. Tell me everything that's happened since I've been gone."

"It's been . . . interesting," I said vaguely.

"Interesting? Did you tape that program I wanted to see on Channel Twelve? Did you finish that paper you were writing for English when I left? You did pay the paperboy, didn't you? Did you eat right?"

I cut into the flow of questions which, knowing my mother, could go on indefinitely. "Mom, tell me about Ireland." With that, Mr. Donelly caught up with us, and they both started talking at once about all that they had seen.

Maybe tomorrow I'll tell her, I thought to myself. Tomorrow or the next day, just as soon as I figure out where to begin.

JANE MCFANN lives in Newark, Delaware and teaches English at Glasgow High School. Her loves include family, friends, rabbits, Siberian hamsters, ninth graders who do their homework, seniors who like to think, red cars, real smiles, and, of course, writing.

🌀 Avon Flare Romance Novels

THE GIRL OF HIS DREAMS   70599-0/$2.95 US/
Harry Mazer $3.95 Can
Sophie was not part of Willis's fantasy—neither the girl he imagined
for him nor in his plans for the big race—but their romance is a story
dreams are made of.

I LOVE YOU, STUPID! Harry Mazer   61432-4/$2.95 US/
                                                                           $3.50 Can
Marcus Rosenbloom, an irresistible high school senior whose main
problem is being a virgin, learns that neither sex nor friendship—is
ever very simple.

HEY KID! DOES SHE LOVE ME?   70025-5/$2.95 US
Harry Mazer $3.50 Can
Jeff Orloff is ready to put his career dreams on hold for a chance at
the greatest love of all time. But what he can't understand is how a
world-class love like his cannot be enough.

RECKLESS Jeanette Mines   83717-X/$2.95 US/$3.50 Can
Fourteen-year-old Jeannie Tanger discovers the pain and bitter-
sweetness of first love when her romance with school troublemaker
Sam Bensen alienates her from her friends and family.

SOONER OR LATER   42978-0/$2.95 US/$3.75 Can
Bruce and Carole Hart
When 13-year-old Jessie falls for Michael Skye, the handsome,
17-year-old leader of The Skye Band, she's sure he'll never be
interested in her if he knows her true age.

WAITING GAMES   79012-2/$2.95 US/$3.75 Can
Bruce and Carole Hart
Although Jessie loves Michael more than ever, he wants more from
her. Jessie must make a decision. How much is she willing to share
with Michael—the man she's sure she'll love forever?